DANNY ORLIS
FORCED DOWN

DANNY ORLIS FORCED DOWN

BERNARD PALMER

Danny Orlis, Forced Down
© 2024 by Bernard Palmer
All rights reserved. First edition 1972.
Second edition 2024.

Scripture quotations from The Authorized (King James) Version. Rights in the Authorized Version in the United Kingdom are vested in the Crown. Reproduced by permission of the Crown's patentee, Cambridge University Press.

Cover image: Adobe Firefly

Character illustrations: John Ball

Editor: Jon D. Fogdall

Aneko Press Youth

www.anekopress.com

Aneko Press, Life Sentence Publishing, and our logos are trademarks of Life Sentence Publishing, Inc.
203 E. Birch Street
P.O. Box 652
Abbotsford, WI 54405

JUVENILE FICTION / Religious / Christian / Action & Adventure

Paperback ISBN: 979-8-88936-076-6

eBook ISBN: 979-8-88936-077-3

10 9 8 7 6 5 4 3 2 1

Available where books are sold

CONTENTS

CHAPTER 1

THE ACCIDENT

Tom Sparkling Eyes and Raymond White Deer stood uneasily in the snow a short distance from the tense little crowd that had gathered about the mission ski plane. It had snowed at Caribou Narrows the night before. Drifts had piled on drifts until the twin trails of the aircraft were blotted out and the northern wilderness took on a fresh whiteness.

The snowing had stopped at dawn, but the slate gray clouds that blanketed the sun threatened to add to the already deep snow.

"Think they know?" Tom whispered to his companion.

Raymond shook his head. "How could they? No one knows but you and me and Little Joe, and he's scared to tell."

Tom hoped that he was right, but he couldn't be sure. Watching Danny Orlis and the Hudson Bay store manager get the boy with the broken leg into the Cessna 180, he wanted to get out of there fast. Little Joe Nighttraveler was the son of the chief, and that made the situation even worse. Their only hope was in not being found out. Tom trembled at the thought that the crusty old chief might learn they had been responsible for his favored son's broken leg.

"I sure didn't think he was hurt that bad," Tom said aloud.

"Neither did I," Raymond whispered.

Tom scanned the crowd uneasily. "I don't see Big Joe. Is he around?"

"Haven't you heard? He's been sick all week." A sigh of relief escaped from Tom's lips. That was the first encouraging thing that had happened since Chief Nighttraveler's son fell and broke his leg while walking along the river bank several days before.

They hadn't intended to hurt the ten-year-old boy. They had only wanted to taunt him because he started going to visit the new missionary and then made a decision to follow his God. Big Joe and the elders had been furious and would have driven the missionary out if he had lived on the reservation, but he didn't. He had built a house on government land a mile away.

The men were angry with Grady Owens, the missionary, and Little Joe, but the guys Tom's and Raymond's age thought it a huge joke. Big Joe urged everyone to follow the old ways of spirit worship and saw that the tribe had a sun dance on the reservation every June or July. But now his youngest son was a Christian.

Half the guys in the village taunted Little Joe about his decision to walk with Christ. The other half wanted to, but didn't quite dare, in spite of the fact that Little Joe's older brother, Howard, was as vocal as anyone.

In spite of what happened, Tom and Raymond liked Little Joe and hadn't wanted to hurt him when they accosted him on the riverbank. They were only going to torment him a little when they found him alone that day.

* * *

"What did Big Joe say when he found out you weren't going to burn sweet grass and tobacco and have dreams the way he and the rest of the old men do?"

Little Joe colored but did not answer them. He only said, "I've got to go."

"You're not in any hurry. Stick around. We want to talk to you some more," Raymond said, grinning.

"We sure do," Tom said with mock sincerity. "You're a Christian so you should be able to give us a sermon." Laughter came from both boys. "Come on. Tell us all about it, eh?"

Fear darkened the ten-year-old's eyes. "You leave me alone."

"What's the matter? Doesn't that God of yours take care of you? Won't He keep the big, bad boys from picking on you?"

Little Joe retreated warily, half a step at a time. "If you don't leave me alone, I'll tell my dad."

They glanced apprehensively in the direction of the village, as though to see whether Big Joe was coming their way. They were afraid of the fiery chief, but they didn't let his son know it.

"Why don't you tell that God of yours that we're bothering you?" Raymond persisted. "Grady Owens told you that He would take care of you, didn't he? Didn't he tell you that all you have to do is ask God for help and He'll do anything you want Him to?"

The younger boy flinched and edged to one side, trying to gauge how far away he would have to get from them before he could whirl and dash away. Tom and Raymond grew bolder as they saw the fear that they were causing in him.

"Yeah," Tom said, "why don't you talk to God about making us leave you alone? Get down on your knees and pray."

Raymond laughed at the thought. "*That* I would like to see!"

Suddenly Little Joe stopped retreating. He planted his feet firmly in the snow and refused to move although they both crowded close to him. Sweat moistened the wolf hair that lined his parka hood.

Mounting fear made his heart pound and caused his breath to come in short gasps, but he would not move.

"Come on, Little Joe!" Tom blustered, his voice louder, now that they had pushed their captive farther from the village. "Let's hear a tiny little prayer. Get down on your knees and pray for us."

The boy was frightened, but there was the blood of the chief in his veins. It was wrong to let them make him do something that would give another chance to ridicule the God he now followed. Whatever happened, he had to stand. He could not allow them to push him around anymore.

"*Kawin!*" he exclaimed, his young voice harsh. "No, I will not do it!"

The older boys were surprised by his sudden show of courage. They had not expected that from him, a lad half their size. Anger clouded the once-laughing eyes.

"I said pray!" Tom growled.

When the boy did not move, Tom put both hands on his chest and gave him a shove. He hadn't wanted to hurt him. He hadn't even intended to knock him down. He only wanted to taunt him a bit, to show him that he'd better be afraid of him and Raymond if he knew what was good for him. He wanted to make him see what the people thought of his determination to let Jesus Christ have full control of his life. But Little Joe caught the heel of his mukluk on a rock and fell backward, tumbling off the steep riverbank.

He rolled toward the river. Suddenly a cry of pain escaped the smaller boy's lips.

Instantly the anger and arrogance fled from the older boys' eyes. They both leaped down the bank and knelt beside Little Joe.

"Are you alright?"

Little Joe was motionless. He tried desperately to hold back the tears, but the pain was intense.

"I–I–." He tried to speak, but he could not. The two boys watched helplessly as Little Joe fainted from the pain.

Raymond saw that Little Joe's leg was twisted grotesquely under him. "It's his leg, Tom!" Sudden fear hushed his voice. "We'd better get Big Joe!"

Tom Sparkling Eyes gasped. "Big Joe?" he stammered. "Do we *have* to get him?"

"It'll be worse for us if we don't!"

That was true, Tom acknowledged inwardly. If they didn't go to him now, the chief would be wondering why. And after Little Joe was cared for, he would be around asking questions and expecting straight answers. Tom trembled to think what would happen to him and Raymond if Big Joe found out.

So Raymond, who was faster than Tom, ran to the chief's house to summon help.

Big Joe Nighttraveler had been sick for several days and was so weak he could not get out of bed even though his favored son was hurt. His eyes burned into Raymond.

"Where is Little Joe?" he demanded; his voice harsh with emotion. "What happened?"

Raymond stammered out the answers to the chief's questions, hoping the chief wouldn't press him for too much information. But Big Joe was not even listening. Even before Raymond finished, he was barking out orders.

"Howard!" he cried from his bed near the stove. "Howard! Little Joe is hurt!"

His oldest son came quickly from the next room. When his father used that tone, it was no time to loiter.

"Go with Raymond to see Little Joe. And take a blanket to wrap him in. And you, Becky, go to the Bay and get Nyquist. Tell him to come quick!"

Little Joe's mother spoke up. "I go with Howard and Raymond," she said quickly, pulling rubbers over her mukluks and getting into her parka.

The three of them hurried across the snow to the riverbank where Little Joe had fallen. The boy, now semi-conscious, began to whimper quietly when his mother touched him. She cradled his head in her arms and ran gentle fingers across his cold cheeks. A glance told her that her son's leg was broken. Tenderly she wrapped the blanket about the upper part of his body, taking care to see that his leg was not moved.

Howard knelt quietly beside his younger brother. And, when Little Joe opened his eyes, he wanted to know what had happened. The injured boy glanced quickly at Tom and Raymond and then back at his older brother, but he did not reply.

"What happened?" Howard insisted.

Little Joe swallowed against the lump in his throat, and he inhaled deeply. "I–I fell."

Howard was shocked by the answer. "That's hard to believe. You've always been as sure-footed as a squirrel."

Little Joe's eyes left his brother's face and strayed to the faces of his tormentors. But he didn't tell on them.

"I fell," he repeated.

Nyquist, the Hudson Bay store manager, came at that moment, looked quickly at Little Joe's leg and confirmed that it had been broken.

"We're going to have to get you to Finland House to the hospital," he said gently. "You'll have to have the bone set."

New fear came to Little Joe and he looked quickly up at his mother whose smile was reassuring.

Nyquist took charge of the situation with the calm authority of one who had spent long years in the out-of-doors and had witnessed many accidents. He explained to Little Joe that he had to put splints on his leg to keep it from hurting him worse when they moved him. Then he sent Raymond for a toboggan and Howard to the store for two short crating boards to use as splints and two rolls of bandages from the first aid chest.

Tom and Raymond watched Howard nervously as

they helped get his younger brother up to the house on the toboggan after Nyquist affixed the splints to Little Joe's leg. Howard hadn't said anything, but they both suspected that he guessed that they were involved in what had happened. He knew they had been tormenting his younger brother because he had become a Christian. That alone could have given him a clue.

Of course, they weren't the only ones in the village who had given Little Joe a bad time about that. Even his father had been furious. Howard himself had told the boys how angry Big Joe had been when his brother came home and announced that he was going to live for Christ.

"You should have heard him swear at Little Joe," Howard had whispered, awe and fear mingling in his voice. "And he slapped him on the side of the head so hard he knocked Little Joe down. He's got a black eye, and he's afraid to stay at home for a while. He's afraid of what Dad will do to him."

After the boys in the village saw what Big Joe's attitude was, they began to tease his youngest son about it, taunting him mercilessly because of his stand for Christ. No, Tom and Raymond were not alone in doing that. But they were both there when Little Joe fell.

"Do you think Howard knows?" Raymond whispered when they were alone, and the Hudson Bay manager had hurried to phone for the air ambulance.

Tom shrugged. Howard was their friend. He didn't think he would tell on them, even if he did know. On the other hand, Little Joe was his brother. He would be mad about the boy's getting hurt. And he just might be mad enough to tell his dad what had happened – if he knew.

Although the boys had waited uneasily for the plane to come and now waited for it to take off with its injured passenger for the hospital at Finland House, they began to relax a bit. In a short time the aircraft would leave, and Little Joe would no longer be around to be questioned. By the time he got back, the chances were that all would be forgotten.

CHAPTER 2

"YOU'RE ALREADY A CHRISTIAN!"

Sixteen-year-old Howard Nighttraveler was also watching the activities around the mission aircraft with a certain uneasiness. His dad had just informed him that he was to go to Finland House with Little Joe so he could send back regular reports to keep the family informed of his brother's progress.

Howard didn't like the idea, but he didn't challenge his father. No one challenged Big Joe Nighttraveler. He was chief as his father and his father's father had been chief, and he didn't let anyone forget it.

Howard would enjoy the flying. He always did. And, on most occasions, it would be a pleasant change to go to a larger village like Finland House. Anything would be better than the dull monotony of Caribou Narrows. It was going with that Danny Orlis that disturbed him. Danny was too much like

Grady Owens, the missionary who had gotten Little Joe all mixed up.

That wasn't going to happen to him. He was already on guard against it. But he still didn't like to be around such guys. They made him feel uncomfortable. He wouldn't be around him, either, if his dad hadn't ordered him to.

Howard wouldn't have admitted it to anyone else, but he had been the first member of his family to get acquainted with missionary Grady Owens. When the tall, blond giant first moved to Caribou Narrows there was something about his stately bearing, his booming voice, and congenial smile that attracted Howard.

He was the first to start going to the Bible studies the missionary held in his home. And when Owens talked about sin and the fact that everyone needed to be saved, Howard knew he should confess his sin, but he was proud and kept postponing the decision.

Although he would have fought anyone else who said so, he knew that he was responsible for Little Joe's decision to walk with Jesus Christ. He had taken his younger brother along when he went places with the missionary. Little Joe was in the canoe when they went upstream to hunt with bows and arrows and later when they went fishing with a hook and line.

It had seemed foolish to both of them to catch fish on a stick and a string when it was so easy to put out a net and get a dozen times as many, but the big white man had fun doing it. And when he let them try, they had fun, too.

They always had good times with Owens, whether they were out in the canoe with him or sitting beside the stove in his log shack just off the reservation. But it wasn't the good times that Howard remembered most. It was those occasions when the missionary read to them from the Bible and explained what it meant. During those days Howard wanted to become a Christian more than he wanted anything else in the world.

He probably would have taken a stand for Christ if one of his friends hadn't done it first. He found out then what it meant to be a follower of Jesus. The men all ridiculed George Bear when they found out what he had done, and most of the village turned against him. There were few who would speak to him when they met him on the paths, and fewer yet who would be seen with him. George spent most of his time alone. He didn't seem to mind, but Howard decided right then that he didn't want any part of it.

And when he saw that Little Joe was beginning to ask more questions of the missionary than he thought he should, he tried to talk to him about it. He had to warn him against making the same mistake George had made. He had to make him see what it would be like to become a Christian and have everyone else against him.

"You aren't going to become a Christian, are you?"

he asked when they were far enough down the river so there was no danger of anyone eavesdropping.

His younger brother looked away as if very interested in something on the shore. "Why?" he asked casually.

"Because you don't want to do anything so foolish, that's why."

Little Joe did not answer him. Howard feared that he was unconvinced.

"If you become a Christian, you'll never have any fun."

"Grady Owens is a Christian, and he has plenty of fun. He laughs all the time."

"Look at George Bear. Everybody makes fun of him."

"I don't."

Howard's anger flared. "You heard what Dad said about George, didn't you? Do you want him to take a strap to you? That's what'll happen. If you become a Christian, Dad'll strap you until you change your mind. And that's the truth."

"He wouldn't *really* do that, would he?" The thought frightened Little Joe.

Howard shivered as he suddenly interpreted the expression on his brother's face. "You're a Christian already, aren't you?"

Little Joe's lips trembled. "What if I am?"

"You'd better not let Dad know it. That's all I can say."

But Big Joe had found out, as Howard knew that he would, that Little Joe was spending a lot of time with the missionary, and he talked with him about it.

"That has to stop," he said sternly. "I don't want you to be like George Bear. You stay away from Owens, do you hear?"

Little Joe looked at him quickly and then turned away. But he didn't look away quickly enough to keep his father from seeing the look in his eyes.

"Or have you already let this stranger talk foolishness into your head?"

Little Joe remained silent, looking out the window.

His father jerked him around to face him and bellowed, "Answer me!"

It was then that Little Joe told his father he had confessed his sin and had put his trust in Jesus Christ to save him.

For the moment, the chief could not speak. He was speechless with rage. "You!" he gasped. "My own son!"

"The Bible says it is the way everyone should walk," the boy stammered.

His father stood up impulsively, and Little Joe shrank away from him, half expecting to feel the force of his great fist against the side of his head.

"The Indian walks the way of the Indian!" he roared. "We are guided by the spirits in the way of our fathers and their fathers before them." He stared hard at his son. "Do you hear me?"

Little Joe was frightened, so frightened he had difficulty forcing out the words. But at last he did speak.

"I am a Christian."

The muscles about Big Joe's mouth tightened ominously, and he grabbed the boy by the shoulder with powerful fingers.

"You can't be! I forbid it!"

Little Joe was quivering, but he had to go on.

"I've already done it. I–."

He wasn't able to finish what he was saying. Big Joe's open hand exploded against his face, knocking him halfway across the room. It was all the boy could do to keep from falling.

"I forbid you to be a Christian!" Big Joe repeated. "You are only a boy. You can't know what you are doing!"

"I thought about this for a long time," the boy continued, courage coming with the words. "I knew you wouldn't like it. I knew Mom wouldn't like it. And the people in the village, maybe they won't like it, either. But I have to do what my heart says I should."

Big Joe lurched forward and struck him again, cutting the flesh under Little Joe's eye with his knuckle.

"You! My son!" Every word was filled with contempt. "I am ashamed of you!"

When Little Joe slunk off to bed crying, his father turned to Howard.

"And how about you?" he demanded, the hurt

still thick in his voice. "Have you followed this white man's God, too?"

Howard shook his head, glad now that he had been wise enough to keep from making the decision that would have angered his father so much.

Big Joe nodded his approval.

"I'm glad that I have one son who is wise enough and considerate enough of his family to stay away from the white man's religion."

* * *

Howard knew that Tom Sparkling Eyes and most of the guys in the village were taunting his younger brother for his stand as a Christian. He probably could have stopped it if he had wanted to. A word from him that his dad would deal with those who gave Little Joe a hard time would have been enough to have made them stop or ease off considerably. But the truth was that Howard got a certain amount of satisfaction from it.

This was something that could enhance him in his father's eyes. That didn't mean, of course, that he wanted to see Little Joe hurt. The younger boy was still his brother and he loved him, in spite of everything. Teasing was one thing. Hurting him was something else.

Howard didn't say anything to anyone about it, but he thought he knew how Little Joe had gotten his leg broken. He had seen Tom Sparkling Eyes and Raymond White Deer with Little Joe a short time before, following Little Joe around and calling him names the way they had ever since he became a Christian. It was Tom who had come running to the house to get help after Little Joe had fallen, so Howard figured they were with him when it happened.

It didn't seem likely to him that his brother would have fallen over the steep riverbank and hurt himself. The chances were that he was pushed. And Howard knew who had pushed him.

He felt like grabbing one or the other by the scruff of the neck and choking them until they blurted out the truth. But there wasn't much to be accomplished by that. He could get Raymond and Tom into trouble with his dad, but that wouldn't help Little Joe's broken leg to heal or ease his pain.

If his younger brother wanted Tom and Raymond punished let him tell on them himself, Howard reasoned. Unless, of course, he was too scared. Howard wanted to get to talk with Little Joe alone, but there was no chance. There was always someone around.

He had gone into the house with Nyquist and the boys who were carrying Little Joe, and had stood nervously beside the bed while his dad and the store manager discussed what was best to do. He had wanted to stay at home with his brother, but Big Joe sent him with Nyquist when the Hudson Bay store manager radioed for the air ambulance.

"Then you can come back and tell me when they come for Little Joe," the chief said.

Howard was sure the plane would come in that afternoon. Usually the air ambulance was on its way as soon as the engine could be warmed up for takeoff. But on this occasion, the plane was not immediately available.

"I'm sorry, but the aircraft is weathered in at Red Sucker Lake and has been for two days. I don't know when it's going to be available. Over."

"This lad needs medical attention. Do you have any other aircraft available? Repeat. Do you have any other aircraft available? Over."

"The Royal Canadian Mounted Police have an aircraft here, but I sent them on another call half an hour ago."

Desperation came to Nyquist's voice. "Is there anything else you can do for us? Over."

There was a brief silence. Then the radio crackled again.

"Just a minute. I think there is an aircraft here that might be able to come over and pick him up. I'll check it out and let you know in twenty minutes. Repeat. I'll see if this private plane can come over and get him. Stand by for twenty minutes. Over."

"Roger. And out."

Fifteen minutes later the radio operator called back to tell them that the other plane was available and would be on its way as soon as it could be refueled.

"Roger." The Hudson Bay manager turned quickly to Howard.

"You'd better run back to the house and tell your dad that an aircraft is on its way. And have your mother get some things ready for Little Joe. The mission plane is at Finland House and will come over after him."

Howard repeated the message to be sure he had heard it correctly and hurried away.

CHAPTER 3

SNOWED IN

Big Joe was glad that the aircraft was coming for his son, but he didn't like having to use the mission plane to get him to the hospital.

"First, they steal my son's heart. Now they make us beholden to them. I don't like accepting favors from such people."

"It is good they come," his wife told him. "Have you looked at Little Joe? There is fever in his cheeks. He has to get to the hospital where they can take care of him."

"That's what the air ambulance is for."

"Howard says the air ambulance can't come," she reminded him. "It might be a week before it could get here. You can be angry about their coming if you like. I am glad for them."

He glared at her. "Would they steal the heart of my wife, too?"

Her eyes met his, steadily. "I want our son to get to the hospital."

"So do I," he admitted grudgingly. "But I still don't like it that we have to use the mission plane."

Silence settled in the room. Then the chief said sullenly, "If they think they are going to win my favor by doing this thing for us, they are mistaken. I still want nothing to do with them."

Little Joe's eyes opened and met those of his mother, who was sitting quietly on the bed beside him. He opened his mouth as though to speak, but she laid a finger on his lips for silence. It was not a time for talking when his father's pride was bending.

* * *

Danny Orlis had just gotten the latest weather report and was preparing to take off for Prince Albert and Regina when the radio message came from Caribou Narrows. He didn't really want to make the flight, and if any other aircraft had been available, he wouldn't have. It would mean another delay getting home, and he had already been gone three weeks. But it wasn't possible to turn down such a request, so he topped off the tanks with aviation gas and flew over to Caribou Narrows.

If the call had come in two hours earlier, he could have picked up the boy and made it back to Finland House before dark. But the way it was, he had to stay over with Grady Owens in his little cabin just off the reservation. That wouldn't have been so bad, but a storm crept in stealthily during the night, and when they got up the next morning it was obvious that Danny wouldn't be flying anywhere that day. The wind had roared in from the northwest carrying a double load of snow in its teeth. It blotted out the aircraft that was tied down a hundred yards away, and most of the time it hid the trees behind the cabin.

"It sure doesn't look good," Grady said, standing at the window and trying to peer out through the frost.

"You can say that again. There's nothing we can do but wait." Danny went over to the stove and poured himself another cup of coffee. "That's one thing about flying in the north, and especially in the wintertime. There's no use in getting in a big hurry. Delays like this come all the time."

Grady Owens frowned. "It would be good if we could get Little Joe into the hospital today. That leg looks pretty bad to me."

"Maybe we should go over and see how he's doing if this storm lets up."

"You can go," the missionary told him, grinning crookedly, "but it wouldn't do for me to try it. I was there once yesterday, and the chief told me that I'm not welcome to come back."

Danny wasn't surprised about that. He knew the feeling against the gospel in some areas, and especially when some of the people began to make decisions for Christ. Still, errands like this one could be an opening wedge.

"Maybe he'll feel a little different when we get Little Joe to the hospital."

Grady shook his head. "Not Big Joe. He was furious when the boy made a decision for Christ. It's going to take more than an airplane trip to change him, that's for sure."

Later in the afternoon the storm let up slightly, making it possible for Danny to go over to the Nighttraveler house to see if there was anything he could do for the injured boy. Big Joe's wife came to the door and ushered him in, silently.

"I'm the pilot who's going to be flying your son to the hospital at Finland House as soon as the weather lifts," Danny said, introducing himself.

She nodded. "I know. I saw you come in yesterday." Although she made no further comment, gratitude filled her eyes.

Only then did Danny become aware of the man on the bed, and of the dark eyes glaring at him.

"Hello. I suppose you're Mr. Nighttraveler, Little Joe's father."

Big Joe did not accept the friendliness in Danny's voice. "Did you come for money? If you did, you'll have to see the Indian agent. He'll pay you."

Danny ignored the belligerence in the sick man's manner and went over to the bed, noting that fever flushed the chief's dark face.

"Oh no, I didn't come for money," he said quickly. "I really came over to see if there's anything I can do to help make your son a little more comfortable. Or you, for that matter. I have a few medical supplies in the aircraft's first aid kit."

"Nyquist looks after him," he retorted coldly.

"Come," the boy's mother broke in with a quick, defiant glance at her husband. "I'll show you where he is."

Danny hesitated momentarily, not knowing whether to go in and see Little Joe, increasing the chief's wrath, or to miss an opportunity to relieve some of the boy's pain.

"I think I have something that will help you," he suggested to the chief.

"I get something from Nyquist," Big Joe snorted. "Go with the woman! She won't rest until you see Little Joe!" With that, deliberately, he turned over in bed, facing the wall.

Danny remained motionless until Mrs. Nighttraveler spoke again. "He is in here."

The tall missionary pilot bent through the door and stepped into the tiny bedroom where Little Joe was lying on a crude cot. He was a handsome lad, but small for his age. With his eyes tightly closed, he looked even younger than he really was.

"Is he asleep?" he whispered.

She shook her head. "I don't think so."

"Hello, Little Joe." He pulled up a rough stool and sat down beside the bed.

Little Joe stirred painfully, and his eyes opened halfway.

"I was beginning to think your mother was wrong," Danny told him, "and that you were sleeping."

"Are you a doctor?" The boy spoke so softly that Danny had difficulty hearing him.

He shook his head. "I'm not a doctor, but I'm going to take you to the hospital in Finland House where there's a doctor who'll fix up that leg."

Little Joe grimaced, and it was almost a minute before he could speak again. "When?" he wanted to know.

"Just as soon as it quits snowing." Danny leaned closer. "That leg hurts pretty bad, doesn't it?"

The boy smiled faintly. "It isn't so bad if I lay real still."

"You wouldn't fib to me, would you?"

He did not answer.

"As a matter of fact," Danny continued kindly, "it hurts pretty bad right now. Isn't that right?"

"I guess so."

His mother spoke up. "Mr. Nyquist came over and gave him a shot of something to help the pain, but he said he can't give him very much because he doesn't know when you'll be able to fly Little Joe to the hospital, and he has to have something in case it's a long time and his leg gets to hurting worse than it does now."

Danny nodded. He asked her how long it had been since the boy had been given the last injection, and left a strong pain tablet with her.

"A doctor gave these to me to keep in the plane's first aid kit in case of emergencies. I think it will help make the pain a little more bearable for Little Joe."

"Thank you." She whispered her gratitude. Danny knew it was to keep her husband from hearing.

"I'll stop by the Bay store and talk to Nyquist, so he'll know what I left for your son."

Danny would have remained and talked with Little Joe for a short while, but it was obvious that the boy didn't feel like talking. He closed his eyes and wadded the bed covers convulsively in his fingers.

When the missionary pilot left, Mrs. Nighttraveler followed him to the door and extended her hand mutely.

There was little let-up in the storm the next day or the next. Snow swirled along the ground and piled high in new drifts that built on the ones from only two days before.

Danny stopped at the Hudson Bay Store and talked with the manager who asked the young missionary to take care of Little Joe.

"Somebody goofed and didn't fill my last order for medicines," he said, "so I'm really running low. I haven't got more than a handful of pain killers, and they might have to last another month."

Danny's own supply of medicine was meager, but he could stock up at the hospital at Finland House, he reasoned. So he doled out aspirin and codeine tablets to Little Joe, one by one.

The snow slacked off during the third night, and the following morning only a few small flakes drifted down. The wind had vanished, and the visibility was 750 to 1,000 feet. Danny turned to his host.

"It looks to me as though we can get on our way this morning. I'm going over to the Bay store and find out by radio what the weather report is."

The report was encouraging. It had quit snowing about midnight and the barometer was rising. The forecast was for occasional snow flurries throughout the morning with a high cloud ceiling and little wind. They expected it to clear by late afternoon, followed by colder temperatures.

"Sounds like that's what you've been waiting for. Reverend," Nyquist said.

Danny laughed at the high-sounding title of reverend, knowing that Nyquist had not meant to be unkind. Then he grew serious. He was anxious to get over to the Nighttraveler house and have them get Little Joe ready to go. He wanted to get out of Caribou Narrows as quickly as possible.

He thanked the store manager for the use of the

radio and turned to leave. "I think I'd better get my passenger and be on my way."

"I'll go with you."

When they got over to the chief's house, they were surprised to find that Big Joe had decided his older son should accompany them.

"I want him to send back word how Little Joe is doing," the chief said. "You have room for Howard?" There was a question in his voice, but it was more than a question. It was a command, given by one who was used to giving orders that were obeyed.

"I'll have room for one person besides Little Joe," Danny told him. "If you want your son to go, that's fine with me."

Danny looked in on the injured boy and was surprised to see how much worse he seemed to be. His cheeks were flushed and his lips were parched and cracked. It was obvious that his temperature was beginning to climb. Nyquist noticed it too.

"I think we'd better give him another injection of morphine and an antibiotic. It looks to me like the beginning of an infection."

Danny nodded. He had neither in his kit, but Nyquist probably had them.

"Go ahead and get your plane warmed up," the store manager said. "I'll see that Little Joe gets his medicine and gets down to the plane when you're ready to take off."

Danny left the house quickly with Howard two

or three paces behind him. There was an ominous stillness in the air, a breathless hush that somehow managed to whisper of trouble to come. But Danny ignored it. He already had the weather forecast, which was favorable, and he had a very sick young passenger to get to the hospital.

CHAPTER 4

FORCED DOWN

It was a bitterly cold morning and it took longer than usual to get the Cessna 180 warmed up enough for takeoff. Danny wished the heater in the plane's cabin was better because of his injured passenger, but he knew that Little Joe would not complain. Indian boys and girls learned to suffer cold and hardship very early in life.

At last, the engine heat was almost high enough for flying. Danny leaned forward and motioned to Howard who knew instantly what he meant. Turning, he scurried up the snowy path to the house where Little Joe was waiting. Moments later they were loading him into the aircraft.

Danny taxied slowly to the far end of the packed snow that formed the runway at Caribou Narrows and brought the plane about. With the engine idling, he glanced at his tense young companions.

"You know, guys," he said quietly, "I have a custom of praying before takeoff to ask God's blessing on our flight."

Little Joe closed his eyes as Danny bowed his head to pray, but not Howard. The older boy stared straight ahead, a firm, angry set to his jaw. He wasn't having any part of the white man's religion, even at a time like this.

"Dear God," Danny began. "You know all about our needs today. You know how the weather is this morning, and what it's going to be by the time we get to Finland House. But You make the weather. We ask that You would guide us on this flight. Help us to get safely to the village where the hospital is so the doctor can set Little Joe's leg.

"We just commit ourselves and this aircraft to Your care, loving God. We'll be careful to give You the praise and the honor and glory. In Your name and for Your sake we ask it. Amen."

When Danny finished praying, all was silent for a moment in the cabin of the little plane, except for the pounding of the idling engine.

"Think that'll do any good?" the older boy wanted to know, a derisive sneer in his voice.

Danny checked the instruments again and glanced over at Howard to make sure that his seat belt was fastened. "I know that it does good to pray," Danny told him confidently. "I've had enough experience with prayer to know that it works."

Howard snorted.

"I take it that you don't believe in prayer," Danny said calmly.

"I don't have to ask God or anybody else for help," Howard said proudly. "I can take care of myself."

"I guess I used to be that way too. Then I finally came to the place where I realized that I *couldn't* take care of myself, that I had to have God's help and guidance."

"Not me! I'm going to be like my Dad. He doesn't need God either."

Danny noted that the oil pressure was where it should be, and the engine was warm enough for takeoff.

"Are you OK, Little Joe?"

"I–I guess so." The boy's teeth were chattering.

Snowflakes flecked the windshield and angled past the side windows as the aircraft climbed over the line of spruce and poplar at the far end of the lake and headed south, then southwest toward Finland House. Danny Orlis frowned his concern. He knew that the forecast mentioned brief snow flurries, but there was more snow in the air than he had expected. And the ceiling was crowding lower than when he had first gone out to start the engine.

Flicking on the radio Danny gave the plane's call letters and asked the weather station at Finland House to come in. The crackle of static was all that greeted him. He called for the remote outpost again and again but without success.

This was a new development. He tried to keep from showing his consternation to his youthful passengers. Flying without radio contact wasn't to his liking, especially in weather like they were facing at the moment. He glanced at Howard. He said nothing, but he was watching Danny carefully, searching his features for some indication of fear, or lack of it. Danny tried to act relaxed and confident. It would do no good to let the boys know he was disturbed by his failure to contact Finland House.

He flew on for another fifteen or twenty miles before trying to call in once more. Now there was nothing on the radio, not even static.

Danny could not understand. He had checked over the radio carefully just before leaving Fairview. That was something he always did, making sure it was functioning perfectly. It had been working well on the way into Caribou Narrows. He had been in touch with Finland House all the way. It wasn't likely that it would go out without some advance warning of difficulty. But, as with any mechanical or electronic equipment, there was always the chance that something could go wrong.

Howard was watching him as he switched off the radio. "Is there something wrong?" he asked nervously.

Danny shrugged. "There seems to be some problem with our radio, but it shouldn't create any trouble. We should be in Finland House in an hour." He didn't mention the snow that was increasing steadily, or the head winds that were developing. He hadn't lied to Howard; the radio being out shouldn't make any difficulties for them, and they should be at Finland House in an hour. Still, he would feel a lot better if the weather would improve.

Howard settled back in his seat and closed his eyes, relaxing slightly. He was taking comfort from the fact that Danny didn't seem to be particularly disturbed. The injection of morphine that Nyquist had given Little Joe was working well. He had been asleep most of the time they had been in the air.

Danny said little as he flew for the next half hour. The weather worsened progressively. The wind was increasing in velocity until the aircraft bucked and pitched its way along, and at times the snow was so thick they had difficulty seeing the ground. All the while the cloud cover pressed lower and lower. He hoped Howard didn't notice that he had to keep dropping lower and lower until finally they were flying at a scant 400 feet.

The boy paid little attention to it until they hit a particularly rough stretch of air and, in spite of his seat belt, Howard had to hang on with both hands.

"It's getting worse, isn't it?"

"It's not getting any better," Danny acknowledged, reaching for the radio phone again. "I'd like to get Finland House and see what conditions are like there."

"I thought our radio was busted!"

"Maybe the operator there was busy or something." Danny did not want Howard to panic. Besides, he reasoned, it just might work.

He tried to call Finland House, but without success. Then he switched to another frequency and tried. Still there was no answer.

"There *is* something wrong with our radio, isn't there?" Howard demanded.

"I'm afraid so." Danny glanced at the dials in front of him. The needle which indicated the power supply stood at zero. Then he detected a faint, sweet odor. "She's burned out a resistor," he told Howard. "That explains why we couldn't send or receive."

Even as Danny spoke, he saw the opaque wall of snow ahead. He banked sharply.

"What is it?" Little Joe cried from the rear of the aircraft where he was lying. "What's the matter, Danny? Why did we turn around?"

"It looks as though we're going to have to go back," he said quietly, "or go around. We can't fly into a storm like that. We'll run the risk of crashing."

Flying with the wind was smoother, but a moment later Danny realized that heading back was not the answer to their problem. The weather had closed in ahead of them and was moving in behind them, as well, until they were all but swallowed up by it.

The wind seemed to shift and began to buffet the Cessna 180 violently. Little Joe cried out in pain.

"What are we going to do now, Danny?" Howard asked, fearfully.

Danny did not answer him. He prayed silently, quickly, for God's help. He had to get out of the air and get out fast. The storm was moving in on them so rapidly that in another few minutes he might not be able to make it at all.

If only he could radio their position, it wouldn't be so bad. But he couldn't do that. The radio was out, and there was no other way to let people know where he and the boys were and what was happening.

Frantically Danny scanned the rough bush country below. A few minutes before they had been flying over a number of lakes. He remembered thinking what a good place that would be to make a forced landing, if it should come to that. Now, however, there was nothing within his range of vision but trees–trees, and a narrow, twisting river. He looked up and down the narrow band of water, trying to see the telltale splotches that would indicate open water.

There was no open water that he could see. And he didn't see a straight stretch of river, either, that was long enough to land on. And, too, there was always the danger of boulders camouflaged by snow. He couldn't see any of those, either, but that didn't necessarily mean they weren't there.

"What are you going to do?" Howard asked. He tried to sound unconcerned, but he gripped the seat tightly.

For an answer, Danny pointed to the river below. Three or four miles ahead he saw a straight stretch of river that appeared to be long enough to land on, and the unbroken band of white indicated that the ice beneath the snow was solid.

"We'll land down there," he said aloud, "and wait this storm out."

Inwardly he murmured a prayer of thanksgiving to God for providing a place for them to land. Tightening his grip on the controls, he angled down to it.

The wind was blowing even harder by this time, and great billowing clouds of snow swirled along the line of trees on either side of the river, occasionally blotting them from view. The snow pushed up at them, and the howling wind jerked the light aircraft one way then another as Danny fought to ease the plane in.

He would have been successful had the wind not seized the plane an instant before touchdown and threw it violently. There was a splintering sound mingled with a sharp report like the crack of a rifle. The aircraft lurched to one side.

Little Joe cried out, pain and terror mingling in his voice. Danny cracked his head sharply against the doorpost. His senses reeled, and for a long moment all went black.

There was no sound in the 180 except the howling of the wind. Howard stared at his companions. His lips moved, but no sound came out when he saw Danny, his head twisted grotesquely to one side and blood oozing from a long, mean gash on his forehead. On the floor in the back lay Little Joe, eyes wide with terror.

Howard turned to the pilot first, grasping him roughly by the shoulder. "Danny!" he cried. "Danny, are you alright?"

Danny stirred slowly, his mind as blurred and as indistinct as his vision. He must have crashed. And he must be hurt. He was aware of the great, throbbing pain in his head. But he could not remember quite where he was or how he had gotten here. He could not piece the events of the last several minutes together coherently. He closed his eyes once more, trying to shut out the pain and the sudden nausea.

CHAPTER 5

FIGHT FOR SURVIVAL

Danny lay motionless in the cabin of the mission aircraft, exhausted by the fight to remain conscious. His mind was still churning wildly; half-formed thoughts flashed in and out, followed by bewildering snatches of conversation and memory. At first it seemed to Danny that Kay was talking to him, urging him to get up and go out to the airport to fly somewhere. Or was he a boy back home and his dad was trying to get him up to go to school? Dimly he could hear a young voice talking to him out of the baffling confusion and could feel an excited hand on his shoulder. Yes, someone was trying to shake him to wakefulness.

With grim determination Danny fought to still his racing mind and sort out reality. He opened his eyes and tried to focus them.

"Danny!" a frightened voice was crying. "Are you alright? Are you alright, Danny?"

He saw the troubled expression on the boy's face, but he could not remember who he was or why he was with him. Then, slowly, the pieces began to fit together. He remembered first the plane, then Little Joe and his injury. He recognized Howard, and then he remembered the weather, the forced landing, and finally, the crash.

Danny spoke with effort. "How's Little Joe?"

"I–I think he's all right," Howard stammered. "He–doesn't seem to be hurt any."

"I'm not hurt any more than I was before," Little Joe murmured.

"Good." Danny had that to thank God for. Little Joe had been entrusted to him. For that matter, he had the responsibility of both boys.

"I'm glad you're alright," Howard continued, his voice still tense. "You were lying so still for a couple of minutes I was beginning to get awful scared."

Slowly, and with great effort, Danny pulled himself erect in the seat and looked about. They had come to a stop on the narrow river not far from the tree-lined bank. The aircraft was leaning sharply. That meant the leg or ski on the pilot's side was broken, or perhaps both.

The snow was swirling by in great, gusty curtains that blurred the dark shapes of the trees. The wind was bending the jack pine and howling about the damaged plane. The situation was critical, Danny realized.

But at the moment, he had things to do – things that could mean the difference between survival and getting safely into the air again when the storm was over, or tragedy. He had to get Howard to find a somewhat sheltered spot nearby and put up the tent he carried for just such emergencies. And between them they had to get Little Joe over to it and into one of the goose down sleeping bags he had along.

Just sitting up required all of Danny's strength and he sagged against the cabin door momentarily. He had thought he would be able to handle his share of setting up camp and moving Little Joe, but now he realized that there would be little he could do. Howard was going to have to bear the brunt of the heavy work, at least for a while.

He was glad to have the Indian boy with him to be sure the important things were done properly. Things like shrouding the engine with canvas to keep out some of the cold and injecting gas into the oil to thin it enough so he could get the engine started again.

Shaking his head to clear away the confusion so he would be able to think properly, he reached for the lever to force gas into the crankcase. He could not move it. Perplexed, he tried again. It seemed frozen in place.

Danny's head swam, and he ran a shaky hand across his face. The linkage must have broken in the impact, or the pump had jammed. But, whatever the reason, it would not operate.

"What is it, Danny?" Howard demanded. "Is there something else wrong?"

"Nothing serious." And there wasn't, if they could get the oil out of the engine before it congealed. He could do what bush pilots used to do – drain the oil from the crankcase and heat it when the time came to start the engine once more.

"Can you find that toolbox in the back?"

"Sure." The boy turned immediately and reached for the toolbox that had been secured beside the motionless form of Little Joe.

"What's the matter?" the boy with the broken leg wanted to know, tears not far from his voice.

"We're going to get the five-gallon pail back there and drain the engine oil into it," Danny told him, "so we can heat it and make it thin enough to start the engine when this storm is over."

"Oh." Relief was evident in his voice.

Howard, though he had never flown a plane and had seldom ridden in them, had been around bush planes ever since he could remember. He knew the importance of haste and scurried to do what Danny had asked him to do. The blast of cold air as he opened the cabin door set Little Joe to shivering.

"D–Danny," the younger boy stammered through chattering teeth.

"Yes?"

"Do you think we'll get to Finland House? Will we be able to get the plane fixed so it can fly again?"

"I think so," Danny told him, hoping he sounded more confident and reassuring than he felt.

There was a long, strained silence.

"Danny, I don't feel so good."

Pain dulled Danny's senses so much that he had to struggle to talk to him. "I know, Little Joe. As soon as Howard gets back, I'll have him give you another pain tablet. That'll make you feel better."

The boy said no more, but he was breathing heavily. Danny laid his own head back against the seat and closed his eyes. For a moment he lay still. The cold was beginning to force its way through his heavy clothes and, it seemed, into the very marrow of his bones. It would be easy, so very easy, to close his eyes and go to sleep. But he couldn't do that. He had Little Joe and Howard to think of.

While the older Indian boy unscrewed the plug from the engine and drained out the oil, Danny prayed. The situation was indeed difficult. He had filed a flight plan, as he always did, so there would be a search for them when they didn't come in to Finland House. And he was right on course. He was sure of that. There shouldn't be any problem in finding the downed aircraft.

He chilled suddenly as he realized that being on course didn't necessarily mean they would be found. It was difficult to spot a downed aircraft, especially in the wintertime when everything was covered with snow. He had flown searching missions himself and had gone directly over the plane that had been forced down without seeing it. That could quite easily happen to them.

Silently he prayed for God's help and guidance and that He would keep all three of them safe.

Then Danny opened his eyes to see that Howard had finished draining the oil from the engine and was putting the plug back into place. The cold and the force of the storm made working difficult. Once Howard dropped the wrench and had to fumble for it in the snow. But finally the cold, miserable job was finished.

Howard dropped the wrench into the deep pocket of his parka, picked up the pail of oil, and started for the cabin door on the passenger's side of the aircraft. He was so numb with the cold and the buffeting of the snow-laden wind that he wasn't watching where he walked. Indeed, he even had trouble seeing anything except the broad outline of the objects close to him. He caught the toe of his mukluk on the end of the ski and stumbled. His grip loosened, and the pail of oil went over, spilling the precious substance in the snow.

Danny, watching from inside the plane, cried out in dismay.

"What is it, Danny?" Little Joe cried. "What's happened?"

Howard stared mutely at the ground. Then he dropped to his knees and reached out with a heavily mittened hand to touch the ugly black stain in the new snow. He touched it hesitantly, as though trying to devise some means of getting the oil back into the pail again.

Danny knew the agony that Howard felt. He felt it too, as he realized the full import of the accident. It meant that they would have to wait to be found by the search planes. Even if there was something they could do about repairing the ski, he couldn't fly out now. That way of escape was closed to them.

Howard got to his feet and was trembling violently as he opened the plane door a moment later.

"I–didn't mean to do it, Danny," he said, tears clinging to his dark eyes. "Honest I didn't. I didn't even see that ski until after I fell over it."

Danny did not scold the Indian boy. He had been doing the best he could. There was no use in shouting at him now. It wouldn't bring back a drop of the precious oil or change their situation.

"You'd better get in and warm up," he said gently.

The Indian boy stared at him, surprised by the absence of abuse. "Aren't you going to say anything to me for what I did?" he asked incredulously.

Danny managed a thin grin. "I might have done the same thing myself."

The boy climbed into the plane and closed the

door, still shivering from emotion and the cold. "I thought you'd say *something,*" he murmured.

Before Danny could explain, the nausea came back and he closed his eyes against it.

"I sure thought you'd say something to me," Howard continued. "I figured you'd cuss me out for what I did. I sure deserved it."

"What would that accomplish?" Danny asked, when he could speak again.

"I don't know, but I think I'd feel better."

Danny glanced at Howard Nighttraveler. The boy knew the seriousness of the situation, too.

"Maybe I could go for help," Howard suggested. "I'm sure this river goes to Finland House, and it can't be too far away. As soon as the storm lets up, I can go and get someone to come and get you and Little Joe."

Danny shook his head. "It's much better if we stay together. Besides, I need you here, and so does Little Joe."

Desperation raised Howard's voice to an unnaturally high pitch. "But, if we just stay here, we'll freeze to death! We've *got* to get help!"

At that Little Joe began to sniffle quietly.

For the first time Danny spoke firmly to the older boy. "We can't talk that way, Howard. We can't even think things like that. We're in a tough situation, that's true. A guy would have to be stupid not to realize that. But we're not going to give up. We've got to fight, though. But we're going to get out of here – all three of us!"

Howard seemed to draw strength from Danny's determination that everything was going to work out for them. He relaxed slightly. "But what can we do?"

Danny started to answer him, but the pain came surging back. For a moment he feared that he was going to lose consciousness. But he couldn't do that. He had to tell Howard what to do!

After a time he managed to speak. "Right now, we've got to get out our emergency equipment. There's a little tent in the back that will take care of the three of us. It's too bad we can't stay in here," Danny mused. He looked regretfully toward the rear of the plane at the cargo he had taken on before the unexpected flight to Caribou Narrows. There wasn't room for them all there, and the cabin was too drafty and cold. They would have to put up the tent outside. Then he continued his instructions to Howard. "There are three sleeping bags and emergency rations and a first aid kit. We'll have to have all of them."

Before Howard got the tent, Danny had him get a pain tablet out of the first aid kit for Little Joe. The aspirin and codeine tablet would help to blot out some of the boy's pain, at least for a little while.

The Indian boy saw the knot on Danny's forehead and the gleam of pain in his eyes.

"Do you want a tablet too?" he asked Danny.

The missionary pilot hesitated. He wanted to take

one of the pain tablets. He knew the relief it could bring. He thought that he had suffered a concussion from the blow on his head, because there was too much pain for anything less. But he could not permit himself the luxury of one of the pain tablets. There was no knowing how long they would be on the river or how long Little Joe would have to lie without having his leg set. No, the boy needed the pain tablets more than he did.

"I'm all right," Danny said. "Maybe you'd better get that tent up, Howard. It looks as though the snow is beginning to let up a little, and we want to take advantage of it."

Howard went out into the still swirling, driving snow, and set to work. Under normal conditions it would have been simple for him to put up the tent in a few minutes. That was something he had grown up doing. They always took tents along when they went hunting or fishing. But trying to set one up in a near blizzard was something else.

He battled valiantly with the canvas until, at last, he got it up and had it securely tied to the nearest trees. Taking the ax from the emergency kit, he cut a good supply of spruce bows to lay on the snow in lieu of a ground cloth for the sleeping bags. When everything was ready, he came back to the plane for Little Joe.

"Here," Danny said, "I can help you a little with him."

But Howard shouldered him aside. "You're going to have all you can do to get yourself over to the tent. I can lift Little Joe easy. I've done it lots of times."

Danny would still have tried to help Howard, but as he moved, he realized that what the boy said was true. Stumbling through the deep snow the short distance to the tent was one of the most difficult things he had ever done. Twice he fell and it was all he could do to get to his feet again. At last, however, he got to the tent and crawled into the goose down sleeping bag, his teeth chattering. He had to wait until he was warm before he was able to tell Howard to break out a can of meat and heat it over the little fire he had built.

"Now, that's the best news I've heard all day," Howard explained in a feeble attempt to joke.

"Me too," Little Joe said. "I'm awful hungry." When they had eaten, they all felt better. Danny lay back in his sleeping bag and closed his eyes. He didn't know how long he had lain there when he heard a weak voice calling his name.

"Danny. Danny."

"Yes?" He turned over on his side to see Little Joe staring at him.

"Danny, are you awake?"

"Sure." He spoke just loud enough to be heard above the wind. "What is it?"

"How long do you suppose we'll be here?"

Danny waited a moment before answering. "We

filed a flight plan," he said at last, "so the search planes will be out looking for us as soon as the storm is over. I don't know for sure. We may be in Finland House some time tomorrow."

Little Joe lay back and closed his eyes. He was quiet for so long Danny thought he had drifted off to sleep, but instead he spoke again, uneasily.

"Danny, I was just wondering something."

"Yes?"

"I was just wondering if you would pray with me tonight?" His voice broke. "I'm scared. I'm awful scared."

Closing his eyes, Danny prayed with the Indian boy. He asked God to ease the pain in Little Joe's broken leg and to help them to get to Finland House as soon as possible. When he finished, Little Joe seemed to feel better. He thanked Danny, and in a moment he was asleep.

Danny didn't tell him that he wasn't the only one who was concerned. He was very much concerned himself.

Night settled in and he closed his eyes in an effort to go to sleep. Back home Kay would be praying for him. That was comforting to him, just as Little Joe found it comforting when Danny prayed for their safety.

As Danny lay there, he began to wonder whether he would ever see Kay again. She seemed so terribly far away – so far away. His mind seemed to carry him backward–.

CHAPTER 6

TROUBLED DREAMS

anny didn't know when or how he first came to realize that he loved Kay and wanted to marry her. He supposed it started when she quit going with him because he was resisting the will of God. That was during his second year at Bible school, and he had been so upset then that he couldn't study and was scarcely able to sleep. He knew then that she had become more than a very good friend to him.

Once he had given his life completely to the Lord and they were dating again, their relationship took on new importance for both of them. In the early weeks of their third year at Cedarton Bible Institute they were engaged. They had planned to be married as soon as school was out.

In those days they spent a great deal of time talking about the future, and what they would do with it.

"You know, Kay," Danny told her one evening,

"God has been laying the field of Guatemala on my heart a great deal lately. In fact, I've been thinking more about it every week. Do you suppose He's leading us in that direction?"

She smiled. "I've been praying about Guatemala for a year, Danny – or have you forgotten?"

He smiled. He knew that was true. It had been one of the factors that had come close to breaking them up the year before.

"If that's where God wants us," he continued, "then, that's where I want to go."

She reached out impulsively and squeezed his hand.

That Christmas he had given Kay her ring. By that time, they had been verbally engaged just over a month. But it didn't lessen the thrill and the joy of that moment. She had gone home with him to the Angle to spend the Christmas holidays. After they had finished the little service that was always a part of Christmas Eve at the Orlis home and had opened their gifts, Danny and Kay went for a walk in the cold night air.

It had been a bright evening. Danny saw it again in his mind. The moon was a sliver in the sky, but the stars, countless thousands of them, seemed to blanket the Angle with light. They pressed so close to the trees and the snow that it seemed one could reach up and take a handful.

Then the northern lights cast their brilliant rays across the heavens. The first appearance was a shimmering stream of yellow and blue, shooting like a silent rocket upward from the northern horizon. While Danny and Kay watched the colors spread, a curtain of light, as multi-hued as Joseph's coat, dropped swiftly and made a graceful curve. After a time, the lights began to fade.

"I've always had the idea that Christ must have been born on a night like this, Danny," Kay whispered, as though the very sound of her voice might break the sacred joy of the moment. "Not the snow, of course, or the forest, or the lake and the creek, but the night itself. It seems as though God made a night like this for a special occasion – perhaps the birth of His Son."

Danny felt the ring box in his pocket. "A night like this was made for other things, too," he told her.

Kay faced him curiously. "What do you mean?" she asked.

It was then that he took the ring from his pocket and placed it on her finger. She gave a little gasp of surprise and joy and moved into his arms.

Danny and Kay were married at the Angle that spring when school was out. For a time, Kay thought she wanted to have the wedding in Mexico where her mother had served as a missionary for so many years. But that didn't seem practical, because none of their friends would be able to come.

Next, she asked Danny what he thought about having it at Cedarton.

"We've both been working in the church there," she said, "and we know a lot of people."

"It would work out fine," he said. "Mother and Dad, and your mother will all be in Cedarton for graduation. We could be married the next day and they wouldn't have an extra trip. And, as you said before, we know a lot of people there. I think it's the logical place."

That was what they decided, but the night before they were to have the invitations printed, Kay changed her mind.

"Danny, what would you think about our being married at the Angle?" she asked suddenly.

"That would be wonderful as far as I'm concerned. There's no place where I'd rather be married than there at home, but I thought we wanted the wedding here in Cedarton so the kids we went to school with could come."

"That would be nice. But, you know, your parents' home on the Angle has been a second home to me ever since I came north to go to high school. If I can't be married in Mexico – and that's certainly not practical for a lot of reasons – I'd like to have it at your parents' place."

Danny took her in his arms and kissed her impulsively. Somehow, it seemed fitting that they should be married in the living room at home. It was the place they both loved the best.

Of course it would mean that a lot of the people they

would like to ask couldn't be invited. There wouldn't be room for them to stay. But the immediate family could be there and some of their closest friends.

There was something else that made Kay's choice of a place for their wedding particularly suitable. He didn't know of a marriage that was happier than that of his parents. Or one that he would be more anxious to model their own marriage after. There was a joy around the house to which people were attracted instinctively.

Yes, he had to agree with Kay. There was no better place anywhere for them to be married than in their own living room.

Danny's sister, Roxie, had been thrilled about the coming wedding, as thrilled as if it were her own. She and Kay spent countless hours together, going over magazines for brides as carefully as though there were going to be a thousand guests instead of the number who could fit comfortably into one medium-sized living room. Danny remembered complaining about the time they spent at it.

"I can't figure out what they could possibly be talking about all the time, Dad," he said one evening when he and Carl Orlis were left alone in the kitchen once more. "They've been going like this for a week now. And it didn't start here, believe me! They were doing the same thing at Cedarton every time they got together. You'd think this wedding was going to take a year instead of twenty minutes. What do they find to talk about?"

Mr. Orlis laughed genially. "That's one thing I've come to accept, Danny," he said, "without ever understanding it. You never question a woman about her talking or her planning. And you especially don't question her about the length of time she takes in arranging a wedding for herself, for her daughter, or even a friend. That's one thing that can take more time than any man can imagine. My advice to you is to stop trying to understand it and simply enjoy it."

While Roxie found the marriage exciting, it was exactly the opposite for her twin brother, Ron. He dragged himself around the house the week before Danny and Kay were to be married, a scowl on his face most of the time. Kay thought he must be angry or ill and asked about it.

"There's nothing wrong with him," Roxie exploded indignantly, "except that he's got it in his head that when Danny gets married it's going to be the end of the world or something."

Kay was disturbed by that piece of information. She was most anxious that everyone in the family would like her. "I'm sorry he feels that way," she said. "I have been hoping he would like me as much as I like him."

"Oh, he thinks you're great. It's just that he's got the idea he won't be able to have any fun with Danny after the two of you are married. The trouble with

Ron is that he's jealous." Her eyes flashed. "Sometimes he makes me so mad!"

Danny realized what was disturbing his brother and tried to talk with him about it the day before the wedding.

"Things aren't going to be any different between you and me than they've ever been."

"Don't try to tell me that." Bitterness crept into Ron's voice. "I know better. They're different already, and it'll be even worse after you're married. You and I will *never* get to do anything together anymore."

"You're mistaken about that, Ron. We'll go fishing and hunting the same as we always have," Danny promised.

However, it seemed that after the wedding, the days flew by and there was no time for Ron. Preparations for the mission field and other responsibilities took all of Danny's time.

* * *

Danny stirred uneasily in his sleeping bag. He opened his eyes, and for a time lay there blinking as he tried to focus them in the darkness. At first, he couldn't remember where he was or how he came to be there, but eventually his senses cleared.

The howl of the wind came into the little tent, driving the cold through the heavy canvas. Danny was warm enough in his sleeping bag, but he knew the thermometer must be dropping to new lows outside.

He turned on his side until he could make out the figures of his youthful companions. They both were sleeping, he was sure. Little Joe, especially, was breathing with the regular rhythm of sleep.

Danny could still see the ugly black stain of the oil against the snow, the oil that was the key to their getting out safely. He closed his eyes once more and began to pray, asking God to take care of them and protect them, to guide them as they tried to master the situation in which they found themselves.

He didn't think there had ever been a time when he had prayed so hard for a physical problem, except for the agonizing hours and days in Guatemala when Kay was so sick. That, too, had been an agonizing time. Again, his eyes closed and he began remembering things that had happened a long time ago.

* * *

Danny had just learned to fly in those days, and they were clearing landing strips at the various mission stations. Kay had been concerned about him and had warned him repeatedly about the dangers of being out in the sun too long.

"You know how dangerous sunstroke is," she told him.

He had been concerned about her, too, and talked

with her a number of times about taking a few days off to rest.

"I will," she told him, "if you'll take off, too. We can go somewhere for a week and forget all about our problems here."

How often Danny wished he had done as she suggested. At least he would have gotten her away for a rest. But looking back was always easier than making decisions at the time. There was flying time to get in, landing strips to clear, and their regular duties to take care of, as well. There didn't seem to be enough hours in the day for them to do what needed to be done.

Perhaps a few days of vacation at that time would have changed the whole outcome of their lives.

But they realized that God was leading them, even in times of trouble.

Finally, Kay had suffered heat exhaustion and there had been times when Danny had feared for her life. He still trembled at the realization that her life had hung so long in the balance. He realized now that God had spared her for a different type of service. How Danny thanked Him for that.

Neither of them, however, had been prepared for the doctor's verdict regarding Kay's health and how it was going to affect their future. When he had finished an extensive examination, he called them both in and talked with them.

"I'm sorry to have to tell you that you can no longer stay in Guatemala."

At first Danny didn't understand what he meant. "Why?" he asked. "Kay's much better now."

The doctor turned to Kay. "I know your heart is here with our people," he said quietly, "and I wish I had some other news for you. Honestly, I do. But the truth is that the heat exhaustion you have just suffered has destroyed your tolerance for heat. You would have nothing but trouble ahead for you if you were to try to stay. And, in the end, you would have to leave anyway."

She stared incredulously at him, unable to comprehend for the moment what he was trying to say. "But I feel all right now," she told him. "A little weak, perhaps, but aside from that I think I feel as well as I have ever felt."

"I can understand that. You have recovered nicely and should continue to make progress, as long as you get to a temperate climate and stay there." He knew the hurt she was experiencing and was as considerate as possible. "You were very close to a heat stroke, Mrs. Orlis. And that, of course, would have been most serious. You're coming along very well, that's true. As I said before, all you have to do is go to a temperate climate and stay there."

Her eyes showed the frustration she felt. "But we can't do that!" she protested. "Our work is down here."

But the doctor was firm in his opinion. "If you

would like to get the opinion of another doctor, I would welcome it, but I'm sure you will find that he will agree with me completely."

Kay hadn't been willing to accept his word alone. In fact, she had insisted on going to several doctors before she grudgingly admitted that perhaps they were right. It was several months before she could reconcile herself to the fact that their ministry in Guatemala had come to an end.

More than once she felt that they should reconsider the decision to work at home. She was feeling so well that she thought she would be able to go back and continue where they had been forced to quit. Once, they had gone back, briefly. She hadn't been there long before she was convinced that the doctor's verdict had been correct. She soon knew that she would be sick again if she continued to stay in the hot, humid country.

But God had given her a new ministry – a ministry as big in its own way, and as important, as the work on any mission field. The decision to take in welfare children and care for them had been made gradually, but with ever-increasing assurance that it was God's will.

It hadn't been because of the money they got for it, although they did find it to be a help. It was the opportunity to reach kids with the gospel who had never heard of Christ before, except in profanity.

Danny always figured that Kay was the one who

had thought about taking in such children. She was so much more sensitive to the needs of others and the opportunities in an area like that. But, whatever the reason behind their decision, it had given them both a rewarding avenue of Christian service.

Kent and Jill Gilbert were the first to come and live with them. Then there had been Linda Penner, the Davis triplets, and of course, Jim Morgan, who first stayed with Danny's parents and later with him and Kay.

Not all of the kids were welfare cases, but Kay had taken them in, finding room in her heart for each of them.

* * *

Danny stirred uneasily in his troubled sleep. He really hadn't given her credit for all she had done. He guessed he was like so many others who took things for granted – until now, when he didn't know whether he would ever see her again or not.

Awake once more, Danny prayed for courage and help. He was still praying when he slipped back into unconsciousness.

CHAPTER 7

"I DON'T UNDERSTAND"

The hours of darkness crept by on ponderous, snowy feet. Morning came reluctantly, inching over the horizon. It appeared stealthily, thinning the dark until it no longer ruled the vast bush country that lined either side of the narrow river.

Danny had regained consciousness sometime during the night and had lain awake or dozed fitfully for several hours. In the predawn light he could only see the outlines of his sleeping companions. A bit later he could make out Little Joe's handsome young features, and he could distinguish the emergency rations and the first aid kit at his feet.

He squirmed over on his stomach and lifted the tent flap to peer out. The dull gray dawn was filled with snow, cold, and driving wind. He had been praying that the storm would let up with the coming of a new day, but it was still as vicious as before. Danny's spirits sagged.

A few moments later Howard asked about fixing breakfast.

"It's about time for it," Danny said.

The older boy crawled out of his sleeping bag and built up the fire again. Once that was done, he melted snow to make tea and prepared oatmeal for them.

At first Little Joe didn't want to eat anything, but Danny insisted.

"I'm just not hungry."

"You'd better drink a cup of tea, Little Joe," Danny said, "and have some oatmeal."

Howard poured a cup of steaming tea for his younger brother and handed it to him. "Try this."

He sipped it reluctantly, but it tasted good. He ate a few bites of oatmeal, slowly. It wasn't long until he had eaten the last of it. After that he felt better.

Danny tried to sit up to eat, but he was so dizzy he had to quickly lie down again. Both Howard and Little Joe noticed it, but they said nothing, even though it was several minutes before Danny was able to eat.

At first Howard tried to keep the fire going. He got up every few minutes and went out to tend it. But the wind and snow made it impossible for him to gather enough wood. It wasn't long until they let the fire go out.

Danny watched Little Joe as closely as he could. The boy did seem to draw some strength from eating, but his cheeks were flushed and his forehead hot with fever. Every now and then he groaned quietly, his thin lips parting to allow the sound to escape.

"What's the trouble, Little Joe?" Danny wanted to know. "Is there something we can do for you?"

The small boy's eyes opened and he looked at Danny pitifully, but he shook his head.

"There isn't anything you can do for me," he whispered. "My leg's hurting awful bad right now. To tell you the truth, I don't feel so good at all."

Danny had suspected that. Little Joe didn't complain, but his face reflected pain.

"Get the first aid kit and bring it to me, please, Howard," he said. "I want to give Little Joe another pain tablet."

Howard silently obeyed. While Danny opened the first aid kit and looked for the pain tablets the older boy hunkered on the spruce bows. He frowned at Danny.

"There's something I can't figure out," he said at last.

"What's that?"

"Why aren't you taking any pain tablets? I can see that you're hurting almost as bad as Little Joe is. Why don't you take one? Is it against your religion or something?"

Danny shook his head. "Like I told you. We don't know how long we're going to be here. Little Joe might need them very much before we get him to the hospital."

Howard still found it difficult to believe that Danny was telling him the truth. Most of the white men he knew wouldn't care whether an Indian boy was in pain or not, and if the man was injured himself, he surely wouldn't endure a lot of pain in order to help an Indian. Oh, there were Nyquist and Grady Owens, who seemed to love the Cree and want to help them. But he wondered if they would really put themselves out to help one of the Indian people the way Danny had.

There had to be some catch to it. There had to be a reason for Danny's being so good to Little Joe. A man just didn't do things like that unless there was something in it for him.

Several times during the day Danny saw that Howard was studying his face seriously, but he didn't ask about it. Howard said nothing more to him. Instead, he kept his questions bottled up inside, pondering over them.

Danny was awake more that day than he had been before. But his head ached harder and his face felt flushed, as though he was getting a fever. He supposed it must be a cold or infection. Whatever it was, he had to fight it if he was going to be able to help the boys. Silently he prayed that God would give him the strength he needed.

Then Little Joe Nighttraveler went to sleep. It seemed to Danny as though Howard had been waiting for that moment, for as soon as the lad was asleep,

Howard turned over to face Danny and began to speak softly.

"You know," he said, "I don't know what makes you tick. You sure aren't like the other guys I know. I still can't figure out why you refuse to take those pain pills yourself."

"I–." Danny started to answer, but Howard interrupted.

"I know the reason you *gave* me, but it doesn't make sense."

"There isn't anything so strange about that. Like I've told you, he's in a lot worse shape than I am, and he's in a lot more pain."

The look in Howard's eyes showed that he was not convinced.

Danny paused thoughtfully. "The Bible tells us that we should have compassion and love for each other and to try to help those who are in need," he said.

"You mean that religion of yours is the reason you're helping Little Joe?"

"I guess you could say that," Danny told him. "The Bible says that God loved all of us so much He sent the Lord Jesus Christ to die on the cross so we can be saved and have eternal life. Because He loved us, we try to love other people in the same way."

"That's another thing I can't understand," Howard retorted. "About God loving everybody, I mean. If He's such a God of love, why did He allow something like this to happen?" Howard's anger was evident, but it was mixed with confusion. "When we were going to take off you prayed that God would take care of us and help us to get to Finland House safely. But what happened? We got forced down and I spilled the oil, and now it looks as though we're never going to get out of here." He stopped, then went on more calmly. "If you ask me, that God you put so much trust in didn't even hear you. And if He did, He sure didn't care much about what happened to us. That's all I can say."

Danny tried to explain to Howard that God's love was different from human love, and that it couldn't always be judged by the present circumstances.

"You see, God doesn't say that He'll give us an easy time or anything like that. And He doesn't tell us that He will answer every prayer in exactly the way we want Him to. He does tell us that He will give us the strength and courage we need to take what comes our way."

Still Howard shook his head. "Maybe you buy that, but I don't. I sure wouldn't want a God who wouldn't help me when I needed Him."

"Maybe God wants to teach us something through the circumstances that happen to us. There are times when that's the reason He allows us to have problems like this."

"You've got it all figured out, haven't you? If things work out good for you, you say God helped you. If they don't you say He's trying to teach you something. Don't try to talk to me about your God. I'm not interested."

Before Danny could answer, the boy went on.

"Then there's another thing. Look at Little Joe. He's got a busted leg and he's a Christian. You're a Christian and you got a knock on the head that just about broke your skull." He grinned arrogantly. "I'm nothing and look at me! I'm the only one who isn't hurt. So, what do you make of that?"

"I don't know whether this is the reason or not, but did you ever stop to think that maybe God kept you from getting hurt because He wants to give you one more chance?"

Howard looked away quickly, disturbed by the tone of Danny's voice and the implication of his words.

"And just exactly what do you mean by that?" he wanted to know.

"Little Joe and I both know where we're going if–if something happens to us," Danny continued. "God has saved us because we've met His conditions for salvation. We have confessed our sin and put our trust in Him."

Howard squirmed uncomfortably. "I don't see what that would have to do with it."

"We have confessed our sins and put our trust in Jesus Christ to save us so we *know* that we would go to heaven. But, the Bible says that you wouldn't.

"Why not?" Belligerence crept into his voice.

"Well, Jesus put it this way. He said, 'unless one

is born again he cannot see the kingdom of God.' He also said that no sinner would ever go to heaven, only those who had had their sins taken away by His own blood." Danny leaned forward slightly. "Did you ever stop to think that God may have kept you from getting hurt so He can give you one more opportunity to become a Christian?"

Howard did not answer. Danny would have said more to him, but he turned his back to Danny deliberately and lapsed into silence. Besides, Danny's head began to swim again, and for a time his mind blurred.

When at last he opened his eyes and looked out he realized that the storm had abated somewhat. There was still a little snow falling, but the clouds were higher, and the wind had gone down. He could see at least a mile up the river. Quietly he breathed a prayer of thankfulness. That meant the search planes could start looking for them.

The second day in the tent was more comfortable than the first. The wind was down and it was warmer, for one thing. For another, the fact that the storm was lessening began to ease their foreboding.

Danny was lying there more asleep than awake when he heard a low whine in the distance. It jerked him to wakefulness as violently as though it had reached out and grasped him by the shoulder.

"What's the matter?" Howard demanded, his voice tightening.

A certain breathlessness gripped Danny as he

strained to separate the new sound from the tense silence of the moment. "Listen!" Danny whispered.

The sound continued, growing louder with each passing minute.

"Danny!" Howard cried, eyes widening. "Danny! Do you hear that? It's a plane!"

"That's right!" Danny's own voice cracked under the strain. And for an instant there was a quick prayer of thanksgiving and desperate hope in his heart. And then he remembered the snow that lay heavily over the aircraft and their tent. They didn't even have a fire built so the smoke could help attract the attention of the searcher.

And then he remembered the flares!

"Howard!" he shouted, "get the flares! Quick!" The boy scrambled out of his sleeping bag and frantically pushed his way through the snow to the aircraft. By this time it was apparent that the aircraft was going to fly directly over them.

"The flares! Hurry!" Danny cried hoarsely.

Little Joe, awakened from sound sleep by the noise and confusion, was frightened. "What is it?" he asked, the words quavering.

"It's a plane," Danny shouted happily.

While Howard fumbled frantically under the seat for the flares the plane came into view. The pilot was looking for them, Danny realized. The plane was following the river and headed toward Finland House. Relief surged over him. They were going to be found and taken to the village where the hospital was located.

It seemed that the pilot in the plane above had seen them. The right wing of the aircraft dipped slightly, as though he was signaling to them, and it looked like he was going to bank and come around again.

Howard thought the same thing and let out a triumphant cry of joy, dropping the flares in the snow. But the plane kept on going, still following the river.

Danny's heart sank within him. He even had the fleeting thought that perhaps God didn't care, after all.

"I blew it!" Howard cried out, miserably, tears filling his eyes. "We could have been rescued, if I hadn't been so dumb!"

There was an air of sadness in the tent as Howard came shuffling through the snow, the unused flares and the flare gun in his hands.

CHAPTER 8

ESCAPE PLAN

Danny Orlis studied Howard Nighttraveler's face seriously. Once more he saw despair in the boy's eyes. Danny couldn't censure him for his mistake. In spite of the fact that he was trusting God to help them get out safely, and kept assuring himself that God was going to answer his prayer, a new sense of dread flooded his mind. They had been so close, so very close to being discovered.

He knew that Howard was blaming himself for the fact that they had not been seen by the search plane, but Danny knew it was not Howard's fault. There had been so little time to get the flares and the flare gun out of the aircraft, for one thing. For another, it was still very possible that the pilot would have missed it, even if he had fired it. Danny tried to tell all this to Howard, but Howard continued to blame himself.

"There's no use trying to make me feel any better about it," he blurted. "I know who messed things up."

"Don't be so hard on yourself," Danny told him. "Anyway, if one plane is looking for us, we can be sure there will be others. And this time we'll be ready for them. We'll have the flare gun and the flares here in the tent, and as soon as we hear the drone of the motor, we'll get outside so we can fire the flare."

Howard, however, was not willing to accept the fact that they would have another opportunity to signal a search plane.

"There's no use kidding ourselves," he said, "there isn't going to be another search plane over here. They've got so much bush to cover looking for us that they'll never come this way again."

Little Joe was listening intently, his cheeks flushed and the muscles about his mouth pulled taut with pain and emotion. Danny saw the panic in the boy's somber eyes and the way in which he searched Danny's face for some indication of his own inner thoughts about their situation.

"If we were far off course that would probably be true," Danny said aloud. "But they're going to give our course a good combing."

He had spoken without conviction. Actually, what he said was more of a hope than a firm belief that it would happen. They were on course, that was true, but the searchers wouldn't know that. And Danny hadn't been able to radio their position at the time they had to go down. If he had, they would concentrate on their approximate location, but now the entire area would have to be combed.

Not only that, but it would be difficult to see the aircraft in the snow. He knew that from experience. He had been on search missions himself and knew how hard it was to spot a plane when there was even a little snow cover.

Little Joe seemed satisfied with Danny's assurance that the search planes would find them, but not Howard. He exaggerated the seriousness of their position. His hands were working nervously at the zipper of his sleeping bag.

"We've got to figure out some way of getting out of here," he exclaimed, his voice rising. "If we don't, we're all going to die!"

Little Joe caught his breath sharply at that, and Danny expected him to start to cry. He warned Howard to silence with a stern glance that could not be misunderstood. The boy sat back, sullenly staring at the ground. He said no more, but it was easy to see that his emotions were near the surface.

The inactivity was getting to Howard – that, and the feeling that there was nothing they could do to help themselves. Danny knew this was something that had to be dealt with now, before the situation got any worse, before Howard exploded into some rash action.

"Did you ever help work on aircraft, Howard?" he asked with a suddenness that startled both boys.

Howard looked up at him quickly. "I've never done any more than help with the tying down of planes that came in to Caribou Narrows to stay the night or put in gas. Why?"

"I think maybe you can give me a little help." He unzipped his sleeping bag. "Give me a hand, Howard."

"What for?"

"I'd like to go out to the plane with you and take a look to see what needs to be done to that ski."

"What's the use?" the boy protested, almost belligerently, as though it was Danny's fault that the aircraft had been damaged in the forced landing. "We can't do anything with that."

"We'll never know until we go out and try." Danny said firmly.

Little Joe's eyes brightened hopefully, but Howard doused the hope with bitter scorn.

"And, even if we did get the plane fixed so it could take off and land again, we'd still be stuck here. We can't fly without oil, that's for sure."

Danny paused. What Howard said was true. They couldn't fly the aircraft without oil for the motor, even though they might be able to fix the ski. Still, there was a strange thought creeping into his mind, a thought so vague that it could scarcely be called a thought at all. It was more of a feeling that there was something he could do. It seemed as though there was something he had heard of happening to an old-time bush pilot years before, something very similar to what happened to them, only he couldn't quite remember what the veteran pilot had done to get by without the spilled oil.

It hurt Danny's head even to try to think. Grimly he tried to force the problem out of mind and to concentrate on getting out to the plane. He got to his knees, unsteadily, but could not pull himself upright without help. Reluctantly Howard came over and gave him the assistance he needed.

"We can go out and look at the plane if you want to," the boy retorted grudgingly, "but it won't do us any good. I can tell you that right now."

Danny inhaled deeply as spots and dark blotches appeared before his eyes. He grasped the boy's arm for support.

"We're never going to be able to get out of here alive!" Howard continued dismally.

"Take it easy," the pilot whispered harshly, "or we'll have a hysterical boy on our hands."

Howard fell silent, but his lips were trembling as he guided Danny through the snow.

Leaning heavily on the sixteen-year-old, Danny managed to get over to the Cessna 180 and, for the first time, to survey the damage. He thought the ski had been broken, but it proved to be intact. Instead, the leg on the pilot's side had given way under the impact, breaking cleanly off some six or eight inches above the place where it fastened onto the ski.

"This doesn't look as bad as I thought it would be," he said. "I think maybe we can fix this."

Howard laughed mockingly at him. "This I've got to see."

"We'll make a splint like Nyquist fixed on Little Joe's leg. There's antenna wire in the aircraft, and you can cut a couple of short timbers about five inches in diameter."

Howard helped Danny back to the tent and into the sleeping bag. Then he picked up the hand ax and disappeared into the bush.

"Where's he going, Danny?" Little Joe wanted to know.

"To get some timbers so we can fix the plane."

"Is that going to do us any good?" the younger boy asked. "I mean, what about the oil Howard spilled?"

"We'll have to see about that," Danny said, "but right now, we're more concerned about getting the plane repaired so it can fly."

Little Joe eyed him curiously. He knew that the aircraft couldn't fly without oil, but he didn't ask Danny what his plan was. At the moment he didn't want to know. He wanted desperately to believe that the missionary pilot did have a plan, that there was a way he could lubricate the engine so they could get into the air and on to Finland House.

While Howard was in the bush, they heard another

search plane in the distance. Danny tried, weakly, to get out of his sleeping bag and get the flare gun. Nausea shook him so violently that he had to give up. But he realized it wouldn't have made any difference if he had been able to get the flare gun and fire it into the air. The searching plane came within hearing distance, but that was all. He had gone on his way without ever coming into view.

Little Joe listened breathlessly for a long while after the plane went beyond their hearing and all was silent once more. He didn't say anything, but Danny saw that the boy's cheeks were stained with tears.

Having the second plane come so close without even seeing it was discouraging, Danny had to admit. He had read about people who were forced down who saw and heard search planes every day without once being seen by the searchers. He had known of other cases similar to that in which they found the damaged aircraft and the bodies when the snow melted away in the spring. And pilots on the search had said they must have flown over the area half a dozen times without spotting the plane. He couldn't blame Little Joe for being disturbed.

A few minutes before, Howard had taken the hand ax and disappeared into the brush. He was getting the pieces of timber Danny wanted when he, too, heard the plane. He stopped what he was doing and stared upward, trying to catch a glimpse of it against the dark overcast. Maybe Danny would be able to fire the flare gun in time!

Howard was suddenly alive with new hope. He listened for some change in the sound that would indicate the plane had changed course and was coming nearer. But he heard no such sound. Shortly the noise disappeared and despair overwhelmed Howard once more.

He knew what he should do, he told himself. The way things were, there wasn't going to be a chance of getting out alive. He had been to Finland House a number of times, going by canoe in the summer. He thought that the river led to the village. He should start out for Finland House himself, whether Danny said he should or not.

He probably wouldn't have to go all the way to the settlement to get help. There would surely be trappers' shacks along the river. There always were. He could find a place like that where there was food and wood enough to keep him alive until somebody found him. Or, maybe there would even be a trapper in one of them and he could get help for Danny and Little Joe, too.

The temptation to leave was strong within him and once he even took a few steps, angling toward the river some distance from the downed plane so Danny wouldn't see him. Then he paused, looking about, trying to make up his mind what to do.

The only thing that would keep him there was

Little Joe. He couldn't leave his brother, whatever happened. He would never forgive himself if he did go off and Little Joe wasn't able to make it, too. He wouldn't be able to face the wrath of his dad, either. That was another factor. Big Joe would expect his oldest son to take care of his youngest.

Now Danny was another consideration. Howard didn't want to see the missionary die. Even though he didn't like him very much, he didn't want any harm to come to Danny. But he couldn't see staying there and risking his own life for Danny. He didn't mean that much to him.

The thought of leaving Danny made Howard feel guilty. The pilot had made the trip to help Little Joe. Danny wouldn't be in this mess if it hadn't been for Howard's injured brother. Grimly he fought against the feeling of guilt.

The chances were that Danny wouldn't die if Howard left. On the other hand, it might even be the means of saving him. He would get to the village as quickly as he could and send someone out for Danny.

He stooped to pick up the timbers. As he did so, another thought came to him – something so simple that he marveled that he hadn't thought of it before. He straightened slowly, staring into the distance. That was it! The answer to his dilemma!

He couldn't go off and leave Little Joe, but he wouldn't have to. He would make a small toboggan, just large enough to put his brother on, and pull him where he was going. He couldn't take both Danny and Little Joe, but he would be able to manage his younger brother. He was light, and on a toboggan he could move easily. At least he could take him as far as the nearest trapper's cabin. He could cut plenty of wood for him and get the food that was always in the trapper's cabins in the north so Little Joe could eat. And he'd melt enough snow for him so he would have all the water he needed.

And, when he and Little Joe were safe, he would tell the Indian agent or somebody about Danny so they could get a plane over to pick him up. That would work out better for all of them than waiting here until they ran out of food and starved to death, or Little Joe died of fever and infection. And, if the worst did happen, at least he and Little Joe would be safe!

CHAPTER 9

FAILURE

Howard was so excited now that he had worked out a plan of action that he wished he could dash back to the tent immediately and tell Little Joe about it. That would wipe the fear out of his eyes and put a smile on his face, all right. Little Joe was afraid they weren't going to get out alive. He would soon get over that.

Howard knew, however, that he couldn't go and lay out his plan before Little Joe. Even though Danny might be asleep, he couldn't risk having him overhear. If the pilot found out about it, everything might be ruined. No, he had to keep it from him. The only way he could be sure of that was to keep it to himself until the middle of the night when Danny would be asleep and when the darkness would hide his movements. Then he would get Little Joe onto the toboggan and leave.

It wouldn't make a lot of difference if Danny did hear them after they got started. He was so shaky on his feet that he couldn't follow them, or stop them if he did catch up to them. So there was no problem there.

Hurriedly Howard cut the timbers he needed for the toboggan and hewed them flat on one side. Once that was accomplished, he cut a fairly deep groove for the rope or wire that would be used to lash the timbers together. It was two hours later when Howard finally returned to the tent after secreting the timbers for his toboggan in the brush not far from the bank of the river.

When he finally came back with the timbers Danny sent him for, the young pilot was concerned because it had taken Howard so long.

"That took quite a while, Howard," he said, eyes narrowing. "We were beginning to get worried about you."

Howard felt the color flush his cheeks and was afraid his own nervousness would give his plan away.

"You don't have to worry about me," he blurted. "I can take care of myself."

"You must have had quite a time finding the right timbers. You certainly did a lot of chopping out there."

Howard glared at him. He was about to tell him that he had been cutting firewood, but if he did, Danny would expect him to go out and drag it in.

"What's the matter? Why are you so upset? I

got the pieces you wanted, didn't I?" he demanded defensively.

Danny nodded. "Yes, you got them," he said, "but I didn't expect it to take you so long, that's all."

"You're like everyone else!" Howard exclaimed. "I try to do what you want, and you complain because it took me too long. Next time I'll grab the first piece of wood I see and we'll find out if that suits you."

Danny shrugged. "Don't pay any attention to me, Howard. I'm just a little jumpy, that's all."

Howard ignored his apology. "Are these timbers all right for what you wanted?"

Danny examined them with care. "I think they'll do fine."

"It took a little while to get just what you wanted," Howard lied. "I knew they had to be good pieces if they're going to do what you want them to do."

Danny would probably have tried to shape the splints himself, but he thought it would be better to have Howard do it. At least that would give the boy something to do for a time and would help to dispel that feeling of helplessness.

Under Danny's direction Howard cut away one side of each timber until it was flat and would fit smoothly against the broken leg of the aircraft.

"That looks fine," Danny said at last.

"You aren't going to try to put them on this afternoon, are you?" Howard asked.

Danny squinted up at the sky. In an hour it would

begin to get dark, and he still had to have Howard cut a timber twenty feet long, and a short piece to use as a fulcrum so they could raise the aircraft enough to make the repairs.

"There isn't time to do that this afternoon. I think we'd better wait until tomorrow."

Tomorrow? Howard Nighttraveler grinned. By tomorrow, he and Little Joe would be long gone. They wouldn't be around to work on any aircraft. But he couldn't let Danny know that. By this time Howard was convinced that he had the only plan that would keep any of them alive. If he didn't go to Finland House and get help, no one would be saved.

He found an excuse to go out to the plane shortly before dark and found a roll of antenna wire Danny had in the aircraft. He had been looking for a length of rope to use to fasten the logs of his improvised toboggan together, but the wire would work just as well. Better, perhaps. He looked about quickly, as though half afraid that Danny was looking over his shoulder, watching every move. Then he stuffed the wire in the pocket of his parka. He would have to hurry so he could get the toboggan together before dark. Now that he had decided what to do, he was anxious to carry it out.

Howard thought there was more food in the aircraft than Danny had told them about. He figured the pilot had lied to them and was saving something back for himself. But a careful search turned up nothing. That meant he would have to steal some of the food in the tent.

He wouldn't take it all, he decided. It might take two or three days for him to get back and he didn't want Danny to go hungry. He would just take enough so he and Little Joe would have plenty. He would leave the flare gun and the .22 rifle. That would give Danny a chance to signal if any more search planes flew over. And with the rifle he could kill a rabbit and get something to eat.

Howard worked as rapidly as he could on the toboggan, wiring the logs together. In spite of the fact that he worked quickly, it was almost dark when he finished. Danny frowned at him curiously when he finally came back, but he said nothing to him. And Howard was glad that he didn't. It meant that he didn't have to lie to him.

That evening, as usual, Howard built a fire for cooking and to warm the tent a little. They had finished eating, and Danny was lying there enjoying the warmth when he started suddenly.

"What's the matter, Danny?" Howard demanded. For an instant he feared that Danny had surmised what he was going to do and was about to talk to him about it.

"I've been trying to think of something for the last couple of days. I once heard about an old bush pilot who flew in the north about twenty-five years ago. And I just thought of it – what he did when he was in our situation. I think maybe we can get out of here tomorrow."

Howard stared at him incredulously. They might be able to repair the leg on the 180. Howard would acknowledge that that could be done. But flying without oil was a different story.

"What do you mean, get out of here tomorrow?" he said irritably.

"I mean *fly* out of here," Danny said, excitement in his voice.

"Now you are off your rocker. I spilled all the oil. Remember?"

"That's just what I was thinking about. I'll tell you more later."

Howard Nighttraveler was furious. He knew there was no way the plane could fly. But Danny had some scheme, and he wouldn't tell him what it was. Perhaps, Howard reasoned, he remembered some oil that he had stored in the cabin of his plane.

If there was oil in the plane, he mused, it was hidden better than Howard thought anything could be hidden in so small a space. He had gone over the cabin of the 180 carefully himself – so carefully that he was sure that there was no oil there. There was only room to hide a quart or two, and that wouldn't be enough to do them any good.

Maybe Danny had some butter or margarine to melt down for lubricant. As soon as he considered that he realized how ridiculous it was. Margarine or melted butter wouldn't have enough lubricating qualities to get a plane off the ground. And besides, who would carry that much of either one on a regular flight? No, it had to be something else.

Howard shook his head wonderingly. And then he realized what Danny's reason for secrecy must be. He didn't really have a plan at all! He must have been wondering why Howard was gone so long out in the bush that afternoon, and again when he went out to the aircraft just before supper. Danny must have guessed that he was getting ready to rig up something for Little Joe to ride on so they could leave. And he had thought of this fake scheme to keep them from doing it.

Well, Howard told himself, Danny couldn't fool him. He had made up his mind that he was going to get his brother on the toboggan and take off. No one could stop him!

For the first time, Danny had a time of Bible reading and prayer with Little Joe that night. Howard listened disdainfully. If that missionary thought he was going to make him change his mind about leaving because of a page or two out of the Bible, he didn't know Howard Nighttraveler very well. It would take more than that to stop him.

They let the fire die out, and soon Danny was asleep. Howard lay there quietly for another fifteen or twenty minutes. Then, satisfied that Danny was sleeping soundly, he crawled out of his sleeping bag and pulled on his mukluks and rubbers., His pulse was hammering fiercely, and his breathing was quick and shallow. He wasn't afraid, but he couldn't relax until he had Little Joe on the toboggan and was safely away.

"Little Joe!" he whispered in his brother's ear. "Little Joe!"

The injured boy awakened with a start and would have cried out, but Howard had clamped his hand over his mouth.

"Sh! It's me! Howard! Don't say anything! Just listen!"

Hurriedly he told Little Joe what he had planned. "But–."

"Sh!" Howard whispered hoarsely into his brother's ear. "I'll be back for you in a couple of minutes. OK?"

Little Joe squirmed painfully in his sleeping bag until he could see the dark shape of Danny's shoulder. Howard planned to take him and go to Finland House, leaving Danny behind! In a way he was tempted to go along. He was beginning to despair of ever being seen and rescued. It wouldn't be long until the search planes would give up, and then they would have no hope of getting out alive. But as much as he wanted to, he couldn't leave his new friend behind; not when Danny had been taking him to the hospital when they were forced down, and had taken such good care of him. There was a hot flush in Little Joe's cheeks as he struggled inwardly with his decision.

At that moment Howard brushed against the outside of the tent. Little Joe was supposed to be ready for his brother to pick him up and put him on the crude toboggan.

Howard expected Little Joe to be ready and to put an arm about his neck when he knelt silently beside the sleeping bag in order to make it easier to lift him. But instead, he kept his young body stiff.

"No," he said aloud. "I don't want to go!"

"Sh!"

But it was too late! Danny was already awake.

"What is it? What's the matter?" he demanded quickly.

"Come on, Little Joe!" Howard snarled angrily. "We've got a long way to go!"

"I'm not going without Danny!"

"Howard? What's this all about? What's going on?" Danny's voice was louder and clearer as he became fully awake.

"You keep out of this!" the older boy said irritably. "You've caused us enough trouble already. It's none of your business what we do!" He turned to his brother. "Are you coming with me, Little Joe, or do I have to make you?"

"I'm not going anywhere without Danny!" Little Joe declared.

"We'll see about that!" Howard reached down to pick Little Joe up, but before he could move a step a powerful flash of light stabbed him in the eyes, paralyzing him momentarily.

"Stay right where you are, Howard!" Danny rasped, directing the beam of light at Howard's face. "Little Joe's not going anywhere, and neither are you!"

Reluctantly the older boy laid his brother back on the pine boughs.

"Now," Danny said coldly, "suppose you tell me what this is all about."

"Take that light out of my eyes," he said, "and I will."

CHAPTER 10

A NEW IDEA

Howard went back to his own sleeping bag and sat down, trembling with anger and fear. When Howard did not offer any explanation of his actions, Danny reminded him that he was listening.

"Just start at the beginning," Danny told him coldly, "and tell me exactly what you planned to do."

"I wouldn't have tried it if you'd do something to help us get out of here," he blurted accusingly. "But you won't! You're going to let all three of us die, that's all!"

"Go on. I still haven't heard what I want to hear."

At Danny's insistence Howard told him about the toboggan he had made and how he was going to put Little Joe on it and pull him along the river until they got to Finland House. "Or to a trapper's cabin where we could get in out of the cold and have a fire. But we weren't going to leave you here, Danny. We were going to send someone back for you just as soon as we got to the village. Honest we were."

Danny was silent for a short time. When he spoke his voice sounded sad and tired. "Howard, take this flashlight and go to the plane and bring me the charts."

"What do you want the charts for?" Howard asked.

"I'll show you when you bring them to me."

Danny turned over on his side and raised on one elbow, shaking away the mental cobwebs. When Howard returned, Danny spread the chart beside his sleeping bag and had Howard train the beam of the big flashlight on it.

"I'm going to show you something, Howard," he said. "Here's where we are." He indicated a spot on the river. "But there are a couple of things you apparently aren't aware of."

"Like what?" There was scorn in his young voice.

"For one thing, this river doesn't go to Finland House. I filed a flight plan calling for this course because it passed over the new lake and stream. With the weather so uncertain I wanted to be close to a spot where we could set down if we had to."

Howard bristled. "You can't tell me that! I've taken this river to Finland House. Don't forget I've lived in this territory all my life."

"I know that, Howard. But this is a brand new chart, only six months old. Look here." Danny pointed to the chart. "There's a new man-made lake right here – thirty miles this side of Finland House

– that's changed the whole terrain. It's like a whole new country on the other side. Besides, it's changed the course of this and several other small rivers that once went in that direction."

Howard swallowed hard. "I didn't know that."

"The other thing is that this is a trapping preserve. You'll find it marked on some maps."

"A preserve–."

"So, if you had gone off with Little Joe, you'd both have been in big trouble. As I recall, it's at least eighty miles down this river before you come to a settlement, and for most of that distance you'd be in the restricted trapping area. You wouldn't find any trapping cabins, because there just aren't any trappers."

Howard was too ashamed to make a reply or even look at his brother or Danny. He sat quietly staring at the tent floor.

Danny's voice became kind. "The only hope we have, Howard, is to stay together and try to help each other as best we can."

"I guess you're right," he mumbled.

"I do have a scheme to get our plane into the air again, but I can't do it alone, Howard. I didn't want to say too much earlier because I didn't have it all worked out. I didn't want you to get your hopes up. And as things are, there's little that I can do except to tell you what to do. Will you help me?"

"What choice have I got?" he asked, shrugging indifferently.

"You can leave if you want to," Danny said. "There's nothing I can do to stop you."

"I know. But I'll stay."

Silently Danny thanked God for Howard's decision. He knew he could trust Howard to do as he said he would.

Later that night Little Joe spoke softly. "Danny? Danny?"

"Yes?" He shook himself to wakefulness. "What is it?"

"I was just thinking something."

"Yes?" Danny asked.

"God really watched over Howard and me tonight, didn't he? We'd have been in terrible trouble – a lot worse than we're in now – if we'd run off and left you the way he planned to!"

"Yes," Danny replied, "we can thank God for watching over all of us tonight and for keeping us from doing something very foolish."

"Why don't you say what you mean?" Howard cried angrily. Danny did not know that Howard had been listening. He jumped in surprise at the sudden outburst. "Why don't you come right out and say that I goofed again? Everything wrong that's happened on this trip has been because of me!"

"I can tell you this much," Danny said calmly, "if it hadn't been for you, Little Joe and I would be in a lot worse condition than we are now. And that's for sure."

Howard was still not convinced. "What makes you say that?"

"Neither one of us has been able to do anything. We've had to depend on you. And tomorrow, when we try to fix the plane so we can get it in the air, we're going to have to depend on you again."

Howard's voice brightened. "I'd never thought of it that way."

"Maybe you haven't, but it's true just the same." Then the boys fell asleep, but Danny lay awake for a long while praying silently, asking God to help them get the plane repaired and into the air again.

The following morning, he was already awake when Howard crawled out of his sleeping bag and started to make a fire.

"You'd better move it out a ways," Danny told him, "and make it bigger than what we've used before."

Howard's gaze met his, full of questions. "How come?"

Danny's eyes were laughing. "Suppose you do as I say. I'll tell you when everything's ready."

"I don't see–."

"I don't want you to think I'm completely crazy. If I tell you the whole thing now, you'll never believe me!"

While they were eating breakfast Little Joe turned to Danny with his question. "I can see how you're going to fix the leg on the plane, but what are we going to do for oil?" he asked seriously.

"This is going to sound crazy to you both, but I

finally remembered a story an old bush pilot told me about what he did when the same thing happened to him. He was hauling fish in the wintertime and was taking the oil out of the motor so he could heat it on the stove when he was ready to fly the next morning. That was back in the days before planes had devices to inject gasoline into the oil to thin it down for easier starting in subzero weather. He stumbled and spilled his oil the way Howard spilled ours."

"Big deal," the older boy muttered.

"Wait until I'm finished. He looked at that oil-stained snow for a couple of minutes and finally decided that all he had to do was get the snow and the oil separated and he could heat it and put it in his engine."

The boys stared at him in disbelief. "You don't expect us to believe that, do you?" Howard said, trying not to laugh.

"It won't hurt to try it and see. We'll pick up a little of the snow and oil at a time and heat it in one of our bigger kettles. When we've melted the snow and warmed the oil, we'll strain the water out of the oil through a shirt and we should be in business again."

Howard frowned thoughtfully. "Do you suppose it'll work?"

"I'm convinced of it. The oil got stiff the instant it touched the snow so it didn't even spread over much of an area. Since it's by the plane, not too much will have been blown away. Unless I'm badly mistaken, we'll be able to recover most of it – at least enough to lubricate the engine until we get to Finland House."

Hurriedly, Howard Nighttraveler set to work. It was simple to find the place where the oil had been spilled, but heating the oil and snow and separating them was slow and painstaking. The process was working, there was no doubt of that, but it consumed far more time than Danny had supposed it would. The morning was gone by the time they finished with that part of the task, but the boys were jubilant.

"What do we do now?" Howard wanted to know.

"We've got to lift the damaged side of the 180 and get it blocked up so we can splint the ski leg," Danny said. He glanced up at the sunless sky. "And we're going to have to hurry if we don't want to spend another night here and take the risk of another storm catching us."

Danny thought he would be able to help Howard, but he soon found that he couldn't. He managed to get halfway to the plane before he stopped and went back. He had Howard cut a long pole to use as a bar and a short length of log to use as a fulcrum. Then he had him get a longer length of log on which to set that side of the plane.

"Just how am I going to do all of that alone?" Howard wanted to know.

"Get that piece of antenna wire and I'll show you."

Howard colored slightly. "I'll have to take it off my toboggan," he said. "That's what I used to tie the timbers together."

Danny showed him how to arrange the logs so that they could be used as a fulcrum and lever. By using the principle of leverage, Howard could lift the damaged plane alone.

"Now," Danny said, "tie the end of the wire around the log, right in the middle so you can move it without having it fall over."

Howard nodded. "Then what do I do?"

"Take the free end of the wire around the good ski leg and bring it back to the place where you're standing. Then when you've raised that side of the plane you can pull on the wire and move the log under the fuselage to hold it up."

Danny had to go over that three times with Howard to be sure he understood it. Then the boy set to work. It took him half an hour to raise the plane and pull the section of log under it to hold it up, but at last that was accomplished. Then he cut the splints to proper length, put one on each side of the broken ski leg, and wired them in place as tightly as he could. With Howard's help, Danny managed to get over to the plane and examine the work when it was finished.

"It looks fine," he said at last.

In another hour the engine had been heated with the firepot he carried for that purpose, the oil had been warmed, and they were ready to try to start the engine. Danny bowed his head for a quick prayer asking God's help and reached for the starter. Howard and Little Joe waited breathlessly.

CHAPTER 11

ANOTHER CHANCE

Danny's forehead was covered with beads of cold sweat and his hand was trembling as his fingers sought for the starter. He tightened his grip on the wheel in a futile attempt to keep his head from spinning. He was afraid that he might lose consciousness again.

Panic seized him. If he couldn't keep his mind clear, he couldn't fly. He wouldn't dare take the plane into the air. But did he dare to keep the boys on the ground – especially Little Joe? There was no telling what would happen to the Indian boy if he didn't get to Finland House – and soon.

The injured lad's temperature had been climbing steadily, an indication that the infection in his body was spreading, and once he had been delirious, his mind disoriented by the fever. When he was normal, he lay in silence, without strength enough even to speak, except to answer their questions or to tell them when he wanted something. Danny had to get him to a doctor where he could be treated for infection and have the bone in his leg set. He had no choice if he wanted Little Joe to live.

"Dear God!" he prayed inwardly and in quiet desperation, "You know that I can't take this plane into the air unless my mind is clear and I have more strength than I've got now. Help me!"

Howard saw that there was something wrong, and fear laced his voice. "Danny!" he cried, grasping the pilot by the arm. "Danny!"

"What's wrong?" Little Joe wanted to know, his parched lips blurring the words. "What's happening?"

"I was a little dizzy for a minute," Danny said, "but I'm all right now."

With that he reached out once more and tried the starter. The engine ground painfully.

"Do you think it will start?" Howard asked anxiously.

The motor backfired once and the boys both grinned.

Danny knew that didn't necessarily mean anything, but he tried once more and the engine fired several times and caught! It was running now – slowly – but it was running!

"Praise God!" Danny breathed aloud.

This time Howard had nothing to say.

"I knew God was going to start our engine for

us," Little Joe murmured happily. "I've been praying ever since we got in and I – well, I just knew He was going to start it!"

It was so bitterly cold that it took a long while for the engine to run smoothly and even longer for the engine heat and oil pressure to reach safe levels for flying. But, at long last the aircraft was ready to fly.

Danny forced his eyes to focus and taxied out onto the river and turned into the wind.

"Danny," Little Joe said, "can I pray before we start?"

"Sure thing."

"Dear God," the boy began, "You've taken care of us ever since we left home and we want to thank You for that. We want to thank you, too, for helping Danny to remember about the oil and for helping Howard to get it picked up and put back in the engine. And we want to thank You for helping Howard and Danny to get the landing gear fixed so we can take off.

"Now we're going to fly to Finland House. Dear God, just help us to get safely into the air and not to run into any more storms or things like that. And help us to get to the hospital safe and–."

He continued to pray, talking to God the way one would talk to an old and trusted friend. When he finished Danny glanced at the older brother. He thought he saw tears in Howard's eyes.

"Thank you, Little Joe," Danny said simply.

After a prayer like that, Danny felt great confidence.

He pushed the throttle forward and the aircraft began to gather speed. There was an anxious moment just before takeoff when they hit a patch of very rough ice. Danny prayed silently that the landing gear leg would hold and eased the plane into the air. It came up slowly and for an instant he was afraid it would bounce on the snow and rough ice with disastrous results. But he opened the throttle and the aircraft staggered higher into the air. Thanksgiving and praise to God flooded his being.

"We've made it!" Howard cried aloud. "We've made it!"

Above the drone of the engine Danny could hear the sound of Little Joe's voice. He couldn't make out what the boy was saying, but he knew that the injured lad was also thanking God that they got into the air.

A great unbroken cloud stretched from horizon to horizon and there was a bit of snow in the air, but this time no storm materialized. Less than an hour later Danny touched down on the landing strip at Finland House.

Danny sagged over the controls, his strength gone and his mind reeling. He was still in that position when another pilot who was gassing up to continue the search for them recognized the aircraft and came hurrying over to it.

"Say, now! I'm glad to–" His voice choked off as he saw Danny. "What's the matter with him?" he demanded of Howard.

"He hit his head," Howard said, as he made his way to Little Joe. "And my brother's hurt. Get us some help."

It wasn't long until the ambulance came and took Little Joe and Danny to the hospital. Danny regained consciousness on the way to the hospital, but the strain of the trip had depleted his strength. He was nearly delirious and kept insisting that he was not hurt.

"I'm all right," he told the nurse. "There's no sense in my being kept here. Let me out!"

The nurse tried to quiet him by agreeing. "I'm sure you're right, Mr. Orlis. I know the doctor will be happy to release you. Right now, you're being put in here for examination and observation."

Danny tried the same tactics with the doctor when he came in, but he was soon exhausted and fell asleep. He woke hours later to the sound of the doctor's voice.

"You've had a nasty blow on the head, Orlis," he replied, "and you're suffering from exposure and shock. I've got to have you here in the hospital where I can keep a close watch on you."

Danny was sensible now and asked the doctor to send for the local aircraft mechanic so he could get the repairs made on the 180. The doctor had one of the girls in his office send a radiogram to Kay so she would know that he was all right. Danny wanted to go down and see Little Joe, following his own examination, but the doctor refused.

"He's asleep right now and probably will be for a few hours, so it wouldn't do you any good to go and see him. Besides, my orders to you are to stay in bed, flat on your back, for a few days."

"How is Little Joe?" Danny wanted to know.

"He's got a badly broken leg, and he's full of infection. If it weren't for the antibiotics we've got these days, I'm afraid we'd have our hands full trying to save his life. As it is, I see no real complications."

"Thank God," Danny breathed.

The doctor didn't seem to understand what Danny meant. "Yes, the boy will be in the hospital for a while, but he should get along very well," he said, and then left the room.

Danny lay back and closed his eyes. For the first time since he had taken off from Caribou Narrows with Little Joe and Howard, he was able to relax. He had forgotten what a luxury that was.

Howard came in to see him several times during his stay in the hospital. He didn't say a great deal, but he would sit for an hour in the chair by Danny's bed, staring off into space.

Danny wanted to share Christ with him, but it didn't seem appropriate at the time. It wasn't until he was released from the hospital a week later that he had an opportunity to talk with Little Joe's older brother.

"I went down to see the plane this morning," Howard said. "It's all fixed now and it's ready to go – the leg, the radio – everything."

"I'm glad of that. I was supposed to have been home almost three weeks ago."

There was a heavy silence like a curtain between them. "There's something I've been wanting to talk with you about, Howard," Danny said.

Howard did not respond too eagerly. He thought perhaps Danny still planned some punishment for his foolish attempt to run away.

"Let's go over and have a cup of tea, shall we?" Danny suggested.

They went across the street from the hotel to a little cafe with one table and four stools at a small counter. It was fairly early in the morning, and they were the only ones in the place except the cook.

"Now, what did you want to talk to me about?" the boy asked, grinning nervously.

"You and I had some talks out on the river about Jesus Christ. Have you done any more thinking about Him?"

Howard was relieved, yet apprehensive. "What if I have?"

"God spared all of us, Howard," Danny went on, "but the next time He might not do that."

"What do you mean?"

"He gave you another chance to confess your sin and to put your trust in Jesus Christ. He might not do that another time."

Danny went on to tell him again how much God loved him – that He loved him so much He had sent

His Son to die on the cross to save him. He told him that Jesus Christ wanted to save Him and to give him a new life.

"But He won't force Himself on you. This is a decision that you have to make – and you alone. I can't make it for you and Little Joe can't make it for you. You've got to decide for yourself whether you are going to walk with God or to continue to walk with Satan."

Howard listened restlessly to the familiar phrases. That was the same thing Little Joe had been telling him the last few days. It was the same thing that Grady Owens had told him as long as he would listen.

He wanted to go to heaven, he knew that. But he knew what his dad would say. He wasn't sure he could stand up against Big Joe's anger the way his younger brother had done.

"You think about it," Danny told him. "And, if you decide you want to become a Christian, come and see me before I leave."

"When do you think you'll be going?"

"I'm going to check the plane out this afternoon," Danny said, "and I'll probably leave in the morning shortly after daylight if the weather's OK."

That afternoon Danny went in to see Little Joe to tell him he would be going the next day.

"Know what happened?" he exclaimed, his face radiant. "Howard was just here. He told me that you'd talked to him, and he wants to be a Christian. He was going over to your place as soon as he left here."

Danny's heart soared.

"That's wonderful." He stood quickly. "I guess I'd better get back over there. I don't want to miss him."

"You won't have to worry about that," Little Joe said. "I told him he didn't have to go over and see you unless he wanted to, that he could make his decision for Christ right here."

Danny's eyes widened. "And he did?"

"Yeah! He prayed right here," the boy exclaimed. "Isn't that great?"

Danny Orlis had to admit that it was great, indeed. It was more wonderful than if he had been the one to point Howard to a saving knowledge of Jesus Christ. Now he knew why he had been called to pick up Little Joe and why they had been forced down on the way to the hospital.

"I wonder why Howard waited so long," Danny said thoughtfully.

"He was afraid," Little Joe answered. "My dad hit me when he found out I was a Christian. And when Ray and Tom pushed me–." He stopped suddenly.

"So they did push you. Does Howard know that?"

"Yes, he knows. And he was afraid that the older boys might do something like that to him, too. But he said it wouldn't matter. He said he knows that God loves him, and now, after this trip, he knows that whatever happens will be the best thing for him."

"Right," Danny agreed and gently messed up Little Joe's dark hair.

THE DANNY ORLIS SERIES

The Danny Orlis series, by Bernard Palmer, delivers a blend of adventure, mystery, and suspense through various settings—from the Canadian wilderness to Guatemalan jungles. Danny Orlis, an adept outdoorsman, skilled athlete, and committed Christian, employs his quick thinking, calm bravery, and biblical solutions to confront everyday problems and hair-raising dangers. Early stories focus on Danny navigating school life, sports, and outdoor challenges, while in later books, Danny and his wife Kay provide wisdom and guidance to youngsters facing lifelike situations and challenges. Having sold over two million copies, this series has made Palmer a renowned author in Christian youth literature. Palmer is also the author of the Felicia Cartright series and various other series for Christian youth.

AVAILABLE FROM WWW.ANEKOPRESS.COM